THE CASE OF THE MUTTERING MUMMY

By the Same Author

(MC GURK MYSTERIES)

The Nose Knows
Deadline for McGurk
The Case of the Condemned Cat
The Case of the Nervous Newsboy
The Great Rabbit Rip-Off
The Case of the Invisible Dog
The Case of the Secret Scribbler
The Case of the Phantom Frog
The Case of the Treetop Treasure
The Case of the Snowbound Spy
The Case of the Bashful Bank Robber
The Case of the Four Flying Fingers
McGurk Gets Good and Mad
The Case of the Felon's Fiddle
The Case of the Slingshot Sniper
The Case of the Vanishing Ventriloquist

(OTHER BOOKS)

The Ghost Squad Breaks Through
The Ghost Squad Flies Concorde
The Ghost Squad and the Halloween Conspiracy
The Ghost Squad and the Ghoul of Grünberg

The Case of the Muttering Mummy

A McGurk Mystery

BY E. W. HILDICK

Illustrated by Blanche Sims

Troll Associates

A TROLL BOOK, published by Troll Associates,
Mahwah, NJ 07430

Published by arrangement with Macmillan Publishing Company, Inc.
For information address Macmillan Publishing Company, Inc.,
866 Third Avenue, New York, New York 10022.

First Troll Printing, 1990

Printed in the United States of America.

10 9 8 7 6 5 4 3 2 1

ISBN 0-8167-1789-3

CONTENTS

1   The Mummy Speaks   1
2   "The Curse Has Been Activated!"   9
3   The Carrier of the Curse?   17
4   The Dark Shape   25
5   The Mummy Trap   32
6   The Trap Is Set   40
7   The Face at the Window   48
8   A Composite Mummy?   54
9   Clues—and the Vital Strip   62
10   Donny's Problem   72
11   The Human Lie Detector   79
12   New Evidence   87
13   The Greek Connection   93
14   Mr. Keech Loses Interest   100
15   Breakthrough?   108
16   Differences   114
17   "Eureka!"   121
18   Mari Makes a Call   129
19   Showdown   138
20   McGurk Gives a Pep Talk   148

1 The Mummy Speaks

The mummy was one of the regular exhibits at our local museum. At least the mummy's *case* was. The museum staff used to say that was all there was. With only the *picture* of the dead Egyptian prince— painted on the lid.

Others said that was baloney—that there was a real mummy inside, all right, but badly decayed, with all its cloth bindings rotted and yellow and its bones ready to crumble to dust.

Then there were the wise guys who said *that* was baloney, too. That the case was where the museum staff kept their lunch boxes and purses. Knowing that no one else would dare step beyond the ropes and pry it open, on account of a terrible curse the Egyptian priests had put on that case.

McGurk believed the curse part. He was also one of those who believed there was a decayed mummy in there.

"And it isn't all *that* decayed that it won't get out and walk, one of these dark nights!" he said.

"Oh, yeah?" said Wanda Grieg. "If you think you can scare *me* with that old junk, McGurk, forget it!"

Willie Sandowsky shuddered.

"You really think so, McGurk?"

"Garbage!" said Brains Bellingham, our science expert. "Totally unscientific! As if a few dumb words could bring a dead body back to life!"

Then McGurk turned.

"How about you, Joey? You're our word expert. You're always saying you believe in the power of words."

"Well," I said slowly—I never like to agree too readily to anything Brains says—"I wasn't thinking about *curses*. But, well, sure. There *might* be something in it."

"Absolute total garbage!" said Brains.

"Wow!" gasped Willie. "I got a nasty feeling McGurk and Joey could just be right!"

That was a year ago. Little did we know then that

one day we would be finding out about the mummy the hard way.

It all began when I went to the museum to buy Mom a birthday present. There was a special exhibition on. Its title was on a big poster outside the public library, where the museum is housed:

*FROM
THE JUSTIN MATRAVERS COLLECTION:
EXACT REPLICAS OF OBJECTS
FROM VARIOUS ANCIENT
EGYPTIAN TOMBS*

Well, it didn't exactly sound earthshaking. Replicas aren't the real things, after all. But what did make it special was the fact that Justin Matravers, a millionaire who had recently died, had never put his collection of genuine tomb ornaments on public display. He also made sure in his will that none of his relatives would, either.

But his widow decided to have exact replicas made and put *them* on display. That way the public would be able to get some idea of the fabulous Matravers treasures. And, because she'd been born in our town, she chose our local museum to display them in.

McGurk wasn't impressed.

"Replicas!" he jeered. "A bunch of cheap imitations! I mean, if the *real* ornaments had gone on display, think of the crimes we might have had to deal with!"

Looked at from McGurk's point of view, I guess the exhibition *was* pretty tame. But we went there anyway, one Friday afternoon in early October.

"And those imitations aren't all *that* cheap," I said, as we went up the stairs. "The golden cat is one of the cheapest, and it's gonna cost me eighteen dollars."

Mrs. Matravers had agreed to put an extra number of specimens on sale.

"That will make a very fine gift, Joey," said Mari Yoshimura, the Organization's new member. "Even in Japan we do not always spend so much on presents for our parents."

"Aw, well," I said, "it isn't just a present. I broke one of her favorite ornaments last week—a china cat. So I guess this is the least I can do."

"Never mind about that now," said McGurk. "Let's introduce Mari to Melvin."

"Who, please, is Melvin?" asked Mari, as we stepped into the museum's main room.

"*That's* Melvin!" said McGurk, pointing.

The mummy case was standing near the wall behind the Matravers replicas. They were displayed on pedestals and lighted glass shelves, labeled and

roped off—just as if they were the genuine articles. Things like the golden cat itself—sitting up proud and watchful, right in front of the mummy case—flanked by statuettes of kings and falcons, bulls and hippopotamuses, and crazy Egyptian gods with the bodies of men and heads of birds or crocodiles or jackals.

Mari looked bewildered.

"I do not see anybody where you are pointing."

"That's what all the kids call the mummy," I explained.

"Except there is no mummy," said Wanda. "Just its case."

"Don't be too sure," I said.

"No," murmured Willie. "And keep your voices down. It might be listening."

"Baloney!" growled Brains.

"Forget about voices," said McGurk. "Just keep your *eyes* open, men. I'll be giving you all an observation test when we get back, to see how many items you can recall. You guys are getting rusty."

By now we'd reached the roped-off exhibits. Most of us had started glancing this way and that, trying to get a clear picture of as many items as we could. Mari, however, was staring at the mummy case as if hypnotized by the wide eyes of the faded, painted face.

It was very quiet in the museum. We had all stopped speaking. Joanne Cooper, the museum assistant, was checking some small boxes behind the long glass counter. A guy with a beard was sketching on a pad over on the other side of us. He had eyes only for a statuette of a falcon-headed god. I mean, it was so quiet I swear I could hear the scratching of his pencil.

And then it happened.

The muttering.

The muttering of strange, distant, crackly words. Words traveling through layers of bandages and spices, through molded, painted, varnished wood, through centuries of time.

I strained my ears, anxious to catch every weird syllable. I heard McGurk grunt and Wanda gasp and Willie hiss through his nose. Brains made a faint plopping sound, as if he'd opened his mouth to say something—then closed it again.

There seemed to be no doubt about where that muttering was coming from!

And, as I focused my eyes on those sinister, smiling lips, I began to make out the words that were being muttered.

The mummy had started to speak.

"The Curse Has Been Activated!"

"You are very disrespectful!" came the words, still in that creaky mutter. "And my name is not Melvin. It is Mene-curses, high priest of the great king Amenhotep. *And*"—the creaking became an angry snarl—"if you do not apologize immediately, I will place my most horrible curse on all of you. On you, Jack P. McGurk, with the red hair and freckles. On you, Joseph Rockaway, with the dark hair and glasses. On you, Wanda Grieg, with the long blond hair and wide eyes. On you, Gerald Bellingham, with the short, bristly hair and big glasses and wide-open mouth. And on you, William Sandowsky, with—"

The voice didn't get the chance to describe Willie. Maybe it was going to refer to his long, thin legs and long, thin nose. But, within the space of two seconds, Willie had gotten his long, thin nose safely out of sight. He ran and dove behind the counter.

"Hey! What's going on here?" said Joanne, staring at the sprawling figure at her feet.

Mari darted forward. There'd been a grin on her face, but not now.

"It is all right, Willie!" she said. "I am sorry. I didn't mean to frighten you so badly. It—it was me. *My* voice."

We gaped at her.

"Y-*you*?" said Willie. "But—but—"

"I just could not resist the temptation," said Mari. "I"—here she changed her voice back to the creaky muttering—"I am so very sorry, and I do now re-move all curses."

McGurk had turned very pale, and his freckles

still stood out like dark brown spots. But now he was grinning.

"Sure! Mari's a ventriloquist, Willie! She didn't fool *me* for a second."

The rest of us were beginning to feel pretty foolish. I mean, it had been Mari's skill as a ventriloquist that had helped to solve one of our toughest cases, back at the end of July. In fact, she'd shaped up so well that McGurk had allowed her to become a member of the Organization even when Mari's father decided to stay and open up an electronics factory, and Mari had started school here.

"You're a most valued member of the Organization, Officer Yoshimura," he'd said. "The appointment is permanent."

"What fooled *me*," said Wanda, as Willie picked himself up, "is that Mari wasn't using one of her dolls."

"Me, too," said Brains. "It's really an audio-optical illusion. Focusing the *eyes* of the audience on a dummy to trick their *ears*."

"Only this time I used a mummy," said Mari. "Not dummy. I really am sorry, Willie."

"Now that you've all cleared *that* up," said Joanne, "maybe you wouldn't mind telling me what you think this place is? A museum—or a vaudeville theater?"

"Oh, dear! I owe to you an apology, miss," said Mari. "I so sorry. I got taken away."

She was so upset, her English was slipping.

"*Taken* away?" said Joanne. "If it happens again, you get *thrown out*. Understand?"

But she was smiling. As adults go, Joanne isn't all that bad. Besides, we had once solved the mystery of what had happened to her missing diamond ring, and McGurk was staring hard at it.

"You've still got the ring, Joanne," he said, mildly but meaningfully.

Joanne's smile broadened.

"Oh, all right, McGurk! What is it you want now? Is this another investigation? Because no crime's been committed *here*. Not as far as *I* know."

McGurk looked back at the replicas.

"Nor will there be a crime here. Not with *that* imitation junk! No. We're here on a training session. And Joey wants to buy one of those cats."

Joanne congratulated me as she took one of the boxes from under the counter.

"You're very lucky, Joey," she said. "This is the only cat left, aside from the one on display."

She slipped it from the box and loosened the plastic wrapper. It was about five inches high, sitting up proudly. Its golden coat gleamed.

"Is it *real* gold?" asked Willie, as I turned it slowly around in my hand.

"Of course not!" said Brains. "It's simulated. Didn't you read the notice over there? It's exact in every detail except the original material. Excuse me. . . ." He took it out of my hand and peered closer. "So *this* is travium."

"Travium?" I asked.

"Yes," murmured Brains. "A new alloy. Justin Matravers made his millions out of metals. This was one of the latest alloys to be produced by the Matravers Laboratories. And, boy, it really does look like gold!"

"Correct!"

We all turned. It was the sketching man. His head was going bald, and there were gray hairs in the dark, carefully trimmed beard that hung from the bottom of his chin.

"Furthermore," he said, "travium hasn't been put on the general market yet. This is its first commercial use. Mrs. Matravers thought it would be very fitting to apply it to the collection, since so many of the original items *are* made of gold."

He put out a soft, white hand to take the cat from Brains.

"May I? . . . Thank you." He handled the cat

gently, respectfully. "If this *were* gold, it would cost thousands and thousands of dollars. And even then its value would be peanuts compared to what the original must be worth."

Brains nodded.

"Sure. But everything else is correct. Every measurement, every tiny detail. They—"

McGurk cut him short.

"But if it's such a good replica," he said, addressing the man, "a crook could buy one of these for eighteen dollars and sell it as genuine."

The man smiled.

"Theoretically, yes. But the makers of these replicas are aware of that. So each of the replicas has a stamp on the back—very, very small, so as not to spoil the effect. In the cat's case, it's right here, just at the base, to the side of the tail. See it?"

We crowded around.

"Uh—sure," murmured McGurk.

"I see just tiny scratches," said Mari.

Joanne laughed.

"Here!" she said, taking out a magnifying glass. "This should clarify the situation."

McGurk moved the glass until the faint mark was in focus, then said, "Sure! There it is!"

We took turns peering at the mark. And, since it

was to be so vitally important, I've made this copy of it:

$$\boxed{\text{JMT REPL}_I\text{CA}}$$

And that, too, is an exact replica of the mark, correct in every detail, except for being highly magnified.

"What's JMT stand for?" asked Willie.

"Justin Matravers Trust," said Joanne. She turned with a smile to the man. "Right? I mean, you know much more about . . ." Her voice trailed off. "Is something wrong?"

The man didn't reply. The cat trembled in his hand. His eyes had become glassy, with a lot of white showing. He seemed to want to spin around

toward the mummy case, but something was holding him rigidly in place.

"Oh, no! Please, no!"

We stared.

Under the beard, his Adam's apple was jerking wildly. He seemed to be fighting for air.

Then he shuddered and, with immense care, put the cat on the counter.

"Don't touch it!" he whispered. "Leave it be! Buy something else! One of the falcons. A crocodile. Anything. But not the cat!"

"But *why*?" I said. "I mean—"

"Because," said the man, shuddering again, with the same fearful backward look, "the Curse has been activated! And," he added, in that same, croaky whisper, "if you take that cat away *now*, your life will be in the greatest possible danger!"

3 The Carrier of the Curse?

"But—how do you know?" I said. "I mean—hey! You're kidding, aren't you?"

The man shook his head.

"Believe me, no!" He gulped. "Listen. I do know what I'm talking about. I—I've made a study of these things. My name is Harrison Keech, author of a small book on the subject. *The Funerary Ornaments of Ancient Egypt*. Right, Miss—uh—Joanne?"

Joanne nodded.

"Mr. Keech is making a special study of the Matravers Collection. This is his big chance—"

"My *only* chance," said Keech. "My only chance to get a close look at the collection. Through *replicas*, yet!" He shrugged. "But it's better than nothing. Anyway"—he shuddered again—"I know enough to sense at once what has been triggered here today."

"The curse?" whispered McGurk.

"Yes. A curse. Maybe not the curse *you* were speaking of," Keech added, looking at Mari. "When you made that foolish and terribly dangerous joke. But yes, *a* curse, certainly. I felt it."

"F-felt it?" said Willie.

The man nodded.

"Through the cat. The—the *vibration*."

"But that isn't possible," said Brains, reaching out to the cat. "It—"

"Don't! Don't touch it!"

At the man's hissed words, our science expert snatched his hand back.

The man gulped again.

"I'm sorry! I didn't mean to startle you. After a few minutes, it will be perfectly still. The sensation will have departed. Nobody will ever suspect the curse that will be lurking there, under the surface. But—it *will* be there! Ready to work on you—or you—or you . . ."

He pointed at each of us in turn.

"But why *us*?" said McGurk.

The man took a deep breath. He seemed less terrified, but still very anxious.

"Listen, there is something you have to know. . . . The cat—that cat and all cats—was the sacred animal of the goddess Bastet. The original was probably placed in the original tomb to guard the mummified body."

"Oh, well, that's okay, then!" said Wanda. "I mean, since it's only a replica, and the original mummy is someplace else—"

"No, no, *no*!" said Keech. "No! It doesn't *need* the presence of the original mummy. All it requires is for the spirit of Bastet herself to have been aroused!" He sighed. "Which it obviously was. Aroused by what this child thought of as a joke."

I frowned. "I still don't see how."

The man forced himself to turn and point at the mummy case.

"The mummy in there—or the mummy that once was in there—must have been a follower of Bastet. And the terrible mistake your little friend here made was to put words into that mouth."

His finger trembled as he aimed it at the painted lips.

"I still don't get it," murmured McGurk. "You mean—"

"I mean the priests of ancient Egypt were skilled in the arts of necromancy and sympathetic magic."

McGurk looked at me doubtfully. I shrugged. This guy was losing me.

He seemed to realize this.

"Skilled in the arts of putting life into inanimate objects. And especially dead bodies." Keech turned to Mari. "And one of the most effective methods was by putting *words* into the mouths of dead bodies. Using a form of ventriloquism."

There was a *very* uneasy silence for a few seconds. Mari had closed her eyes tight.

"But—but that's just an old *myth*!" said Brains. "And anyway, how could it put life into *this* dead body? If it isn't even there anymore? Or—or if it *is*—all that's left of it is a few ounces of dust and crumbled bones?"

The man's eyes started to roll upward. His words came out slowly and softly.

"The art of those old priests was great. The power of their incantations could cause the particles of dust and bone to come together again. It could cause the very molecules that were once a living body to reassemble."

Brains was looking thoughtful.

"But dust is dust. How could *anything* make grains of dust come together and—"

"You might as well ask how could anything make small fragments of iron come together again!" snapped the man. "If you were so ignorant that you'd never heard of magnets!"

Brains's mouth hung open.

"Heh! heh! He gotcha there, Officer Bellingham!"

"Anyway," Keech said, "that is how the high priests of ancient Egypt worked their secret miracles. That is how the bodies of their very special followers were reconstituted."

"Like—like dried bananas?" asked Wanda. "Like—uh—dried eggs? Powdered milk?"

"Exactly!" said the man. "And thus become active once again. Active but far more dangerous than reconstituted eggs or bananas or milk." He turned to me. "And so I *implore* you—please, for your own safety—choose some other replica. Anything else. But not the cat."

"Well—"

"Replica though it is," he urged, "it could now be the carrier of the curse. The—the magnet to attract"—his voice dropped—"who knows *what*?"

For a second or two, as I glanced at the cat, I thought I saw it vibrate.

I walked over to the display, wondering if Mom might like one of the hippopotamuses instead.

Something brushed my arm. I jumped—and turned. It was Mari.

"Hey!" I gasped. "Don't *do* things like that to me, Mari! Not *now*! Not after listening to *him*!"

She smiled.

"Joey," she said, in a low voice, "he was only joking. Just as I was joking earlier."

I glanced across. The others were still staring at the cat. The man was saying something else, his bony shoulders hunched, all tense.

"He didn't *look* like he was joking."

"No," whispered Mari. "But I could tell from the sound of his voice."

She looked very sure.

I thought for a moment. After all, Mari had proved over and over that she was a true voice expert.

I smiled.

"Sure, Mari. You're right. I mean, bringing old bunches of dust and bones to *life*! The guy's just got to be joking."

I went back.

"Wrap it up, Joanne, please. I'm taking the cat."

The others murmured. Some sounded approving. I guessed the man had gone on with his spiel just a little too long. Sort of overdone it.

Even he seemed to sense this. His shoulders slumped.

"Oh, well—suit yourself! I tried to warn you, but"—he shrugged, and a smile flitted across his face—"I guess maybe *I* got carried away."

McGurk turned.

"Yeah. Come on, Officer Rockaway. Pay Joanne and let's go. We're wasting valuable training time."

This reminded me to look back as we left. I was hoping to catch sight of a few more objects to add to my test list.

But somehow I never made it. My eyes got no farther than the eyes on the mummy case. They seemed to be following us—me, in particular. All at once, the only thing I wanted was to get out of there—and fast!

4 The Dark Shape

During the next hour or so, we forgot all about our fears.

As soon as we got back to our HQ in McGurk's basement, McGurk hit us with the test.

Okay, okay! I *know*!

He'd warned us. But a lot had happened to distract our minds since then. And the jerk didn't allow any time for the bits to settle.

We were no sooner sitting down at the table— McGurk in his big rocking chair and us on our old, hard kitchen chairs—than he passed out the sheets of paper and peered at the second hand of his watch.

"Right, men! You have exactly five minutes to write down all the exhibits you remember. Starting . . . *now*!"

"Hey, McGurk! I'm not—"

"You have just wasted five seconds, Officer Sandowsky!"

Groans came from all around the table. And no wonder. The results, for most of us, were devastating. Here is the scoresheet that McGurk made me type out.

```
McGurk Organization

Result of Observation test, Friday.

        October 11


Chief Jack P. McGurk          19 items
Officer Grieg                 15 items
officer Yoshimura             12 items
Officer Bellingham             8 items
Officer Sandowsky              6 items
Officer Rockaway               5 items
```

"It isn't fair!" said Brains. "I was too busy trying to get you all to see scientific sense."

"And I got so scared," said Willie, "it shook half of *my* items outa my mind!"

"And I," I said, my cheeks burning, "I had a big decision to make. Whether to buy the cat or something else."

"Never mind the excuses!" McGurk jeered. "You all did lousy. You—"

"I beg your *pardon*, McGurk!" said Wanda.

"Oh, yeah," he murmured. "Except maybe Officer Grieg. Who did—uh—moderate."

"And Mari," said Wanda. "She didn't do too badly, either."

But Mari's head was bowed.

"No, Wanda. Chief McGurk is right. I was so busy listening to the man's voice for signs of—"

"There you go!" McGurk hammered the table. "Excuses, excuses! Real detectives don't make excuses. *Shame on you!*"

Mari hung her head lower. But McGurk wasn't addressing those last words to her. He was glaring at Brains and Willie and me.

McGurk was right. That's what made it so hard to take. My ears were still burning after the evening meal when Willie, who lives next door, came across.

"Hey, Joey," he said, "why don't we put in a little practice?"

"Practice?"

"Yeah. That memory-training game. Where you put all different things on a tray and give the other guy like two minutes to look at them and see how many things he can remember."

"Sure," I said. "Come on up to my room, Willie. I'll test you, then we can go over to your place and you can test me."

Well, Willie didn't do too badly this time, ending with a score of eight out of ten.

"Gee, thanks, Joey!" he said, beaming, when I'd congratulated him. "I feel a whole heap better now. I mean, I really did get a scare this afternoon."

"Sure. Now maybe we can go over to your house and—"

"You bet! I already got a bunch of stuff picked out."

"Good," I said. "I mean, *I* wasn't all that scared. But I was so darned busy trying to make up my mind about the cat—"

"Oh, yeah, *that*," said Willie. "Did you give it to your mom yet?"

"Sh! No!" I said, closing the door. "Not until next week, when it's her birthday."

Willie nodded. Then, as I reached for the door handle again, he said, "Where do you keep it hidden? In here?"

"Where else?"

"Aren't you worried she might find it?"

"No chance," I said. "Come here."

I led him to the clothes closet.

"In *there*?"

"Sure!" I said, taking out a heavy winter coat on its hanger.

I reached under the coat's right shoulder and pulled on the string that was tied to the end of the hanger.

"How about *this*, Willie?"

The cat came out spinning. I had tied the other end of the string to its neck.

Willie stared at it. The glittering spinning movement seemed to fascinate him. His smile faded.

"Uh—yeah—good hiding place, Joey. Only"—a scared look had slunk into his eyes—"put it back now. Huh?"

"What's wrong, Willie? Don't tell me you've started to get the jitters *again!*"

"Well—no—I mean—I don't know. But somehow, seeing it twizzling around made me think of what that guy was saying. About bad vibrations and the curse and stuff."

I laughed. "Anyway, come on. Let's go over to

your place and see how many *I* can score."

It was only half-past seven. And although it was quite dark outside, the lights on our two back porches flooded most of the stretch of yard that we had to cross. So it was all the more of a shock when Willie clutched my arm.

"J-J-J-Joey!"

"For Pete's sake, Willie, what's wrong *now*?"

Willie's face was white in the lamplight. His nose stood out like some kind of signpost.

A signpost that was pointing to the bushes at the end of our yard. To where the darkness began.

And then I, too, saw it.

A tall, dark shape that might have been just another bush. One of those bushes that people cut into fancy shapes—in this case the shape of a bulky, slightly larger-than-life man.

Only we didn't *have* any bushes of that kind.

And then it moved.

Slowly, very slowly. And ponderously. Back, back, back into the regular bushes, merging with the deeper blackness.

If it had come toward us, I don't know what we might have done.

As it was, we ran—ran in the direction we were already headed, into the light of the Sandowsky back porch and through the screen door into the kitchen.

5 The Mummy Trap

Luckily, Mr. and Mrs. Sandowsky were at the front of the house, watching TV. This gave us time to get our breath. Willie brought a couple of cans of Coke from the refrigerator. We gulped it down.

Then Willie wiped his mouth and nodded toward the back door, now firmly locked.

"What—what d'you think, Joey?"

I was beginning to feel a little foolish. I shrugged.

"Mr. Akermann? Walking his dog at the end of *his* yard?"

Willie frowned.

"I didn't see any dog. Or hear it."

"No," I said. "Me, either."

"Yeah . . ."

"So . . ."

I guess neither of us wanted to be the first to say something that might have sounded crazy.

Willie took the plunge.

"Somehow," he said, "that shape looked kinda *bigger* than Mr. Akermann."

"Mr. Akermann *is* a big man."

"I know. But—well—it wasn't that it was a whole *lot* bigger. But . . ."

His eyes had a pleading look as he watched my face. I was trying to recall exactly what I'd seen.

"Bigger in—uh—every direction?" I suggested.

Willie sighed. He seemed to relax.

"Yeah—like—like he was all bundled up. With a kind of helmet—sort of making his head look bigger."

"Like a spaceman?"

"Yeah, but—well—*bundled* up. Not so much a space suit as—as—"

I knew exactly what he was driving at now.

"*Wrapped* up, Willie?"

"Yeah! In bandages. Wrapped around and around with bandages."

I cleared my throat.

"That, Willie, is just the impression I got. But—well—maybe we're letting our imaginations run away with us. Huh?"

An uncertain grin crossed Willie's face.

"Yeah," he murmured. "Sure. . . . I guess you caught some of my jitters. Sorry, Joey!"

I peered out into the night.

"Sure," I said. "That's okay, Willie."

The yards *seemed* clear. Yet all at once those forty feet between his back door and mine looked like forty miles. All thoughts of continuing with the memory game were long gone.

"Look," I said, "I'd better go now. . . . Uh—cover me, Willie. Okay?"

"C-cover you?"

"Uh—yeah. I mean just *watch*. In case—in case it's some—uh—ordinary prowler—or—uh. . . Well, just *watch*, Willie! Please!"

I stepped out, cautiously at first. Then, when I heard Willie click the lock behind me, I walked a touch more briskly.

Anyway, there was no shape there *now*, I thought, reaching the halfway mark and glancing at the bushes. No big, lumbering shape, hampered by heavy wrappings. Only a cat, slowly walking into the lighted area, with its tail in the air. Only—

A *cat?*

Coming from where the dark shape had been standing?

I'd just remembered the goddess Bastet.

My feet hardly touched the ground as I covered those last few yards.

The next morning had already been earmarked for another special meeting. McGurk had told us that he intended to give us an extra-tough training session. But as soon as Willie and I told him of our experience, everything else was forgotten.

"You think it was some kind of prowler?" said McGurk.

We hadn't mentioned anything about our real suspicions yet. Just the thought of *any* old case was enough to arouse McGurk's interest.

"Well—yes. It certainly wasn't anyone we know."

"So why didn't you raise the alarm?"

"Well . . ." I glanced at Willie. "Well, we just weren't sure."

McGurk was scowling.

"What's *happening* to you guys? You're supposed to be detectives. You should have had no hesitation!"

"Yeah—well—you see—we didn't want to be laughed at. Right, Joey?"

"Laughed at?" howled McGurk. "What's that got to do with it when there's a suspected criminal lurking around?"

"McGurk's right, Willie," said Wanda.

"Very true," said Mari.

"One hundred percent true," said Brains.

They weren't just being finks. They really were looking at us with shocked surprise.

"Oh, all right!" I said. "But—well—this wasn't just your common everyday prowler."

McGurk frowned.

"So? Go on! What was it then?"

I took a deep breath.

"The more I think about it—and, believe me, I was awake half the night thinking about it—"

"Me, too!" said Willie. "Tell 'em, Joey!"

"The more I think it was—well—a—a mummy!"

McGurk had been poised in a backward swing of his rocking chair. He came forward with a crash.

"A *mummy*? Did I hear you say a *mummy*, Officer Rockaway?"

"Hogwash!" said Brains.

"Oh, boy!" murmured Wanda.

McGurk turned.

"Be quiet, you two!" His glare simmered down to a glow. "Okay, Officer Rockaway. Tell us exactly what happened, exactly when, and exactly what you saw."

I did this, checking from time to time with Willie, while Brains wriggled in his chair, getting redder and redder and snorting.

When we'd finished, McGurk leaned back with his hands clasped behind his head. He was staring thoughtfully at the ceiling.

"Interesting," he murmured. "Very interesting. If it had been just *one* of you who'd turned in the report, I might have gone along with Brains. But two of you—no."

He leaned forward again.

"Okay, so let's not just sit around saying 'baloney' or looking at our fellow officers like they were nut cases. Instead, let's just use our detective skills to probe this thing."

"You mean the prowler?" said Brains. "Or the mummy garbage? Because—"

"Both!" said McGurk. "Let's do what all good detectives do. Let us assume there could be some truth in what seems at first to be impossible. And let's probe until we come up with some concrete evidence either way."

"That is what scientists do, also, Brains," said Mari. "My father always says—"

But McGurk cut in.

"Let's assume there *could* be a curse. And that the mummy *could* be brought to life. What's the next step?"

He looked around at us with a fierce, triumphant glow.

Brains had been completely silenced by Mari's talk of scientific methods. Wanda, Mari, Willie, and I simply waited for McGurk to answer his own question.

"I'll tell you," he said, beginning to rise from his chair.

"Wh-*what*, McGurk?" whispered Willie.

"We set a trap for it!" said McGurk, standing, leaning slightly forward with his hands on the table, very businesslike.

"A *trap*?" said Wanda.

"For a *mummy*?" said Brains.

"Correct," said McGurk. "A *mummy trap*!"

6 The Trap Is Set

There weren't many people inside the museum that morning. A little girl was saying hi to Melvin, Harrison Keech was sketching, and Joanne was behind the counter. Standing at the counter, half-turned from Joanne, was Donny Towers, her boyfriend. Donny was looking fierce, glaring across at Keech. Donny has a beard, too, but it is a wild, black, barbarian growth compared to Keech's. Think of a vigorous briar patch growing next to a wilting fern.

Anyway, Donny was getting to look even wilder. He ignored our greetings, and it was left to Joanne to respond, with a big, fixed smile.

"Good morning, McGurk! Are you guys wanting to buy some more replicas?" She spoke with a forced cheerfulness. Her eyes looked hard and angry whenever she glanced at Donny. "We're getting in a fresh supply of the cats. They should be here later today."

There was a hiss and a purr. The hiss came through Donny's whiskers—a snorting hiss. The purr came from Harrison Keech, who'd come up softly behind us.

"Maybe they've come to bring the cat *back*, Joanne," he murmured. He was looking at me. "You look pale, young man. Tell me, did you have any strange dreams? Nightmares?"

"No. I—I didn't sleep at all."

"Me, either!" said Willie. "We—hey!"

McGurk had stepped on his toes. He was frowning up at Keech.

"What makes you ask that, sir?"

Keech clucked with impatience. "The curse, of
course! What else?"

There came another snort from Donny.

Keech ignored it. He was staring at me. "Because
I warned you, you know! I warned you what might
happen. And, if I were you, I most certainly would
switch that cat for another, when the new batch
comes in. If you *must* have a cat."

"But what difference would that make?" said
Wanda. "If there is a curse, another cat would still
be dangerous, wouldn't it?"

Keech shook his head.

"No. When the curse was activated, it was trans-
ferred to the cat that was first handled by one of the
offenders. By *you!*" he said, stabbing his pencil at
me. "As I said yesterday, that particular cat will have
been designated as the carrier of the curse. Designated by the goddess Bastet. And the mummy will
be the instrument for carrying out her vengeance."

Suddenly, Brains burst out.

"Pistachio nuts! Impossible!"

"Absolutely!" growled Donny. "Pure baloney!"

McGurk shrugged. He turned his back on the two skeptics and addressed Joanne.

"Have you noticed anything unusual about the mummy case? Does it seem to have changed position or anything? Since—uh—yesterday afternoon?"

"No. Of course not."

But McGurk wasn't put off. He approached the rope barrier.

"Could we take a look inside it, please?"

Joanne looked shocked. McGurk's strange request even made Donny switch his glare for a puzzled frown.

"Inside the *case*?" said Joanne.

"Sure! Thanks, Joanne."

McGurk already had one leg over the rope.

"Certainly not!" said Joanne. "Come back here!"

McGurk looked pained.

"I was only—"

"I'm sorry," said Joanne, "but it's against the rules. And besides, the case has been sealed."

"By the ancient Egyptian priests?" asked Mari.

Joanne laughed.

"No! By the man who used to be the curator here. He used to be bugged terribly by that same request. So he had it permanently sealed."

"When was that?" asked McGurk.

"Oh, a few years ago, when Mr. Mason was curator. The one who—" Joanne faltered. "The one who—uh—died in a car accident."

"When?"

This time the question came from Harrison Keech.

"Well—uh—not long after he'd ordered the case to be sealed." Joanne was looking troubled now. "But you don't think—"

"The meddling fool!" said Keech. "Of *course* there would be a connection! But anyway," he said, turning back to McGurk, "the fact that the mummy's remains are no longer inside the case will make no difference. Even if its ashes were scattered to the four winds, Bastet will have drawn them together again by now."

"But—"

"The case is where *she* resides," said Keech, waving a limp hand toward the case. "The case is now the temporary abode of the goddess Bastet. I can feel her presence. Invisible but all-powerful."

The hush was very deep at this point. Then it was broken.

"Hey, kids!" said Donny Towers, with a harsh laugh. "Why don't you go home and catch the Saturday morning cartoons on TV? Compared to this cockamamy garbage, 'Loonytunes' is higher education!"

"Don't be so rude, Donny!" said Joanne. "Mr. Keech is an expert. He's only explaining one of the ancient myths. That was fascinating, Mr. Keech. Thank you."

Keech bowed toward Joanne. Then, giving Donny a quick, cold stare, he went back to the exhibits and started sketching again.

There was a gritting sound. It was Donny's teeth.

"That guy, Joanne, is nothing but a two-bit . . ."

I couldn't catch the rest. McGurk was steering us toward the exhibits again. With a backward glance at Donny and Joanne, Wanda said,

"Anyway, McGurk, what about the trap?"

McGurk was looking thoughtful.

"That's just what I'm about to set now, Officer Grieg. Uh—Mr. Keech, if the cat that Joey bought yesterday really *is* carrying the curse, the mummy will be attracted by it wherever it goes, right?"

The man frowned.

"Yes. Naturally."

McGurk nodded and turned.

"Okay, so listen, Joey. Why don't you let *me* keep it for a night or two?"

"Hey!" Willie gasped. "Keep your voice down,

McGurk!" He glanced uneasily at the mummy case. "It—uh—she—might hear you!"

"Let her hear!" said McGurk. "If she really *can* make a mummy come to life, she'll now know just where to send that mummy, won't she? What time did you say it was last night, Joey?"

"Just after seven-thirty."

"So that's okay. Seven-thirty is plenty early enough, especially on Saturday. . . . Why don't you guys come around to HQ just after seven, and we'll have a special meeting. Maybe—uh—with a very special guest."

A kind of shivering ripple passed among us.

"And—and if nothing happens?" whispered Wanda.

"If nothing happens, it means we can rule out the supernatural," said McGurk. "Then we'll be able to concentrate on investigating the possibility of a regular *human* prowler."

"Which, if we'd any sense, we'd be doing right away!" said Brains.

"We'll see!" McGurk grunted.

He gave the painted face a grim stare, like it really was some regular human suspect. But even McGurk couldn't outstare those wide, watchful eyes or shake that faint, sneering smile. With a slight shudder, he turned and said,

"Come on, men. We have work to do."

7 The Face at the Window

The work McGurk had spoken about was mainly of a fixing nature: making it right with our parents to give us all a Saturday evening extension to nine-thirty.

This wasn't easy.

Sundown was well before seven, and although there'd been no violent trouble in our neighborhood that fall, some of our parents were very strict about our being out after dark. The fact that one of us, Mari, had nearly been kidnapped had made our parents doubly cautious. It made no difference that the kidnapping had been attempted in broad daylight, in front of dozens of people, months and months ago.

But McGurk fixed it by getting his father to promise that he personally would take each of us home at nine-thirty. Being a McGurk himself, of course, meant that Mr. McGurk didn't do this without squeezing something in return.

"On one condition," he said.

"Sure, Dad! What?"

"That you finally get around to clearing up the leaves, first thing tomorrow morning."

"Aw, Dad!"

"Suit yourself. No leaf clearing, no deal."

McGurk sighed.

"Okay. We'll clear the leaves."

"*We'll* clear the leaves, McGurk?" said Wanda, when Mr. McGurk had gone to make his phone calls. "Don't you know we all have yards of our own, knee-deep in leaves?"

"You heard what my father said," McGurk replied, passing on the squeeze. "No leaf deal, no special Saturday evening meeting."

It didn't seem fair, but he had that very stubborn McGurk look in his eyes. So we agreed.

It was a typical fall evening, rather misty but very still and mild. At first, I thought McGurk was feeling it to be *too* warm. That was when he ordered the last ones to arrive (Willie and me) to leave the door open.

"Wide open, Officer Rockaway. Just close the screen, but make sure the catch is on."

The others were already sitting around the table.

"Did you bring the cat?" McGurk asked me next.

"Sure."

I took the golden statuette from under my shirt.

"Did anybody—or any*thing*—follow you?" he asked.

"Uh—no," I said. My mom had brought Willie and me in the car, and my main thought had been simply to keep her present-to-be concealed.

"Wow!" said Willie. "You think the mummy might be on the scent already, McGurk?"

"I don't think anything, *yet*. Just hand me the cat, Officer Rockaway."

"You'll take care of it, won't you?"

"Don't worry about that."

McGurk was placing it on the table. And when I say "placing," I mean just that.

With *infinite* care, he stood it at a distance of about one foot from the edge of the table, and the same distance from each of the two sides, with its back to him and facing the door. To make quite sure of the angle, he held his head sideways and—using the cat's ears as if they were gun sights—he turned the statuette so that his view of the doorway came plumb between those ears.

"Move a little to the right, Officer Sandowsky," he said. "I don't want you to come in the line of fire."

"L-line of *fire*?" stammered Willie, hastily lurching sideways.

"What I mean," said McGurk, "is if that old mummy comes snooping around, I don't want him to miss his magnet. Or his magnet to miss *him*."

That was enough to set Willie's chair scraping another couple of feet along the floor.

And I have to hand it to McGurk. He was going about this in such a businesslike, confident way that he had us *all* feeling jumpy. Even Brains, who craned his head to make sure for himself that the space between the cat and the door really was clear. In fact, I could swear his hair bristled more than usual when McGurk asked him to move *his* chair, "just in case the mummy takes a peek through the window up there, right behind you."

When McGurk was satisfied that everybody was in the right place, he looked around.

"Okay, men. So now we wait and keep our ears open. But just so we don't waste our time, here's a quiet test." He passed out the paper. "Subject— the museum this morning. I want you to write down exactly who else was present. It doesn't matter if you don't know all the names. Just describe them in as much detail as you can recall."

"But—"

"No buts, Officer Bellingham. I know I didn't give you any warning. In real life you don't get warnings. If those exhibits had been genuine, any one of those grown-ups present could have been an international jewel thief, casing the collection."

Brains's head was already down, his pencil busy. And that went for the rest of us.

Once again, McGurk had shown the power of his imagination. We plunged into that test with such enthusiasm that some of us began to forget about the mummy and the curse.

"Uh—does *Joanne* count, McGurk?"

"Sure! Everyone there at that time, Officer Sandowsky."

"That's dumb!" said Brains. "We know Joanne's no thief."

"Yeah," said McGurk. "But suppose you were a stranger who didn't know anything about her. Then you'd have to rely on your memory. What she looks like, what she was wearing."

Brains grunted. Wanda jeered.

"Brains is only arguing because he can't *remember* what she was wearing. I have five different details already. How about you, Mari?"

"Seven, I think. But first I am describing Mr. Keech and his patterns of speech."

"Hey! That's poetry! Keech, speech!"

"This is an Organization *test*, Officer Rockaway. Not to mention a *stakeout*. Be quiet!"

There was a pretty solid silence for a while after that. In fact, the one who broke it was McGurk himself.

With a gasp.

As we looked up, startled, it was like he was trying to muscle in on Mari's special territory. Hardly moving his lips, just like a ventriloquist, he whispered:

"Hey! Don't look now, but I think I saw a face— up at the window! Sort of . . . white—covered with white cloth!"

8 A Composite Mummy?

I couldn't resist it. I turned and looked up at the window. There was no face there that *I* could see.

As I peered up, I heard the whispers.

"*What* face?"

"Are you sure, McGurk?"

"I'm positive! It was there a second ago."

But although we all stared hard at that dark, oblong slit, nothing appeared. We couldn't hear anything sinister, either.

"Maybe," whispered Wanda, "whoever it was has gone away."

"Yeah," murmured McGurk. "Or maybe he's moving around to the door!"

Crash!

It was Willie's chair, falling as he dashed across to the inner door, leading upstairs.

"Hold it!" snapped McGurk. "I only said *maybe!*"

Then, very cautiously, he got to his feet, walked across to the outer door, reached up and—switched off the light.

"Hey!" gasped Wanda.

"Be quiet!" came McGurk's whispered response.

We were soon able to make out each other's dim shapes. Then a figure loomed up next to me and began to move toward McGurk. It was Brains.

"I think perhaps—" he began.

"Be quiet!" came McGurk's whisper again.

Then I just *had* to get up and follow Brains. The same thought seemed to occur to Wanda and Mari, too. Even Willie had started to tiptoe across from the inner door.

"See anything, McGurk?" I whispered.

He was pressing his ear to the screen.

"I—I'm not sure. I—"

He froze.

Then I heard it.

A slow thudding, slightly above us and to our right. A clumping.

There are five steps up to the yard. The surface of the yard was therefore roughly level with our ears. I felt one of the other guys clutch my shirt as the

clumping drew nearer, still very slowly. A clump
. . . a pause . . . another clump . . .

I was just beginning to wonder which of us would
be the first to break and run, when the clumping
stopped. The last clump seemed to have been about
ten feet away, along the side of the house.

"Is—*is* there someone—out there?" Wanda
whispered.

Brains's glasses glinted.

"Yes—but—maybe only a dog!"

He sounded hopeful, but scared.

"Some dog!" grunted McGurk.

"You know, McGurk," said Brains, "you're acting very—"

He stopped and let out a gasp, a gasp that merged with several other gasps.

We'd heard a muttering. From somewhere beyond McGurk and to our right. A low, angry muttering. In some strange, foreign tongue.

Then I grinned and turned.

"Mari!" I whispered, reproachfully. "*You're*—"

But she was shaking her head.

"Not I, *now*!" she whispered. (And I knew it was the truth because the muttering was still going on.) "And that is not Japanese language, either! Is—is *Greek*!"

Suddenly, the muttering ceased. There was a faint rustling, then the clumping again. But stealthier this time, and faster, and moving away.

McGurk's bravery didn't lapse into foolhardiness. He didn't go barreling out, shouting, "Follow me, men!" He closed the door and locked it.

Then he turned on the light.

His face was very pale. But puzzled.

"Well . . ." he murmured.

Brains, too, was pale. And he, too, looked puzzled.

"If it hadn't been for the voice, I'd have said it was a dog."

"You did say it was a dog," said Wanda.

"I know. A big dog. But—well—the voice . . ."

Brains shrugged, still puzzled.

Suddenly, McGurk's eyes gleamed. He must have missed what I'd said to Mari.

"Officer Yoshimura!" he began.

Mari shook her head so fast that her hair was just a blue-black blur.

"No, no, *no*! I swear! May I lose my ID card if I did throw my voice *that* time! But—"

"Okay," said McGurk. "But it was certainly *someone* doing that muttering."

"Or some*thing*!" said Willie.

Then Brains surprised us all.

"It sure was some*thing*, Willie. It *was* a mummy. A composite mummy."

"A *what*?" said Wanda.

"Sure!" said Brains. "A scientific illusion. Like Mari's ventriloquism."

"You mean—"

"I mean how a ventriloquist gets an audience to focus their eyes on a dummy. Then, when they hear sounds that seem to come from that same distance, they still keep their eyes on the dummy and think that's where the sound's coming from."

"But Mari says she didn't—"

"I'm not talking just about Mari, now. I'm talking

about the way that mummy has been built up in our minds. First: the triggering when Mari *did* throw her voice. Second: Mr. Keech's old fairy tale."

Brains turned to me.

"Next came step number *three*: the dark shape you and Willie saw. By then, your minds were ready to believe *any* dark shape that moved was a mummy. Especially with the cat in your possession. And finally, tonight, McGurk sees something up there that could easily have been a white cat—not even a dog—and everyone thinks mummy again."

McGurk was frowning.

"It did look like some kind of face, though," he murmured.

"Sure! And maybe it was. But—"

"So how about the clumping?"

"Again, that could have been a cat. Pouncing."

"Huh! Some cat!" said Wanda.

"Yeah!" said Willie. "And it could have been a big, white, bandaged *foot*!"

Brains shrugged.

"But then, I admit, it probably *was* a face. The face of some *human* prowler. Some kid, probably. Don't forget, *I* used to snoop around here, before I was a member. When I wanted to join but you wouldn't let me."

A slow grin crossed his face.

"Remember? The time I fooled you into thinking I'd invented a machine to make dogs invisible? And *how* did I do it? By creating an illusion."

This was true. I recorded all the details in *The Case of the Invisible Dog*.

"Officer Bellingham," said McGurk, "you're beginning to make sense! You think some kid's trying to take a leaf out of your book, right?"

"No, no, *no*, Chief McGurk! *Not* child!" Mari sounded very positive. "That was a man's voice. Very, very serious. But strange. And it was saying things in *Greek*."

The old tingle started running down my back.

"Hey! Some of those old Egyptians *did* speak Greek!"

"So—so it could *still* be the mummy!" said Willie.

But Mari was shaking her head.

"No, Willie! This was like the language spoken by man called Dimitri, who works for my father. This was *modern* Greek. Not ancient Greek."

"What was he saying?" I asked.

Mari shrugged.

"Oh, meaningless, really. And strange."

"*How* meaningless? *How* strange?" asked McGurk.

"Well, he was ordering a *meal*. Greek meal."

"*Meal*?" said Wanda.

"Yes. The voice say, 'For starters I will have tar-amasalata. Then I think I will try the moussaka. And I'll finish with baklava and Turkish coffee.' "

We stared at her. This was sounding creepier than even the mummy.

McGurk cleared his throat.

"So—uh—it seems like we're looking for a—uh—normal human prowler after all, men. A very tall, heavily built Greek with a big head, who is slightly cuckoo and likes his food. . . ." He took a deep breath. "Tomorrow, when it's light, we'll see if we can find any *solid* clues out there."

Wanda gave a nervous giggle.

"Yeah! Like maybe a half-eaten hunk of baklava! With *huge* teeth marks!"

Then everyone laughed. Even McGurk.

I guess it relieved the tension.

Whether it would have relieved the tension if we'd known just what *was* waiting out there for us—well, that's a whole other ball game!

9 Clues—and the Vital Strip

As soon as we turned up for the leaf raking on Sunday morning, McGurk announced his plan.

"We start from the perimeter of the yard and work our way toward the sides of the house. That's the most important area, and that's why we leave it to the very last. By then, you should all have your eyes focusing at peak sharpness. Also, the clues near the house are more likely to be footprints in the soft earth and wet leaves. You rake *them* up, and we destroy valuable evidence."

It made sense. It gave us a feeling of closing in. And we did in fact find an assortment of interesting things among the leaves in those outer areas. Like:

- 1 black rubber ball, badly chewed;
- 1 green Frisbee, plus four attached slugs;
- 1 piece of broken red plastic;
- 1 rusty key, about three inches long, mortise type;
- 1 pencil, with broken point, about four inches long, inscribed: *Fast Freddie for Speedy Service, Sal*—which is where the sharpened part began;
- 1 crushed Pepsi can;
- 1 candy wrapper.

Some, or even all, may have had nothing to do with the lurker of the night before. Personally, I favored the pencil. As Wanda pointed out, it looked like a handout from some fast-food place. "Probably a Greek take-out," she said. "Specializing in salads—speedy salads."

"Could be," murmured McGurk. "Anyway, make a note of exactly where you found it, Officer Rockaway."

We did this with all the articles, noting their precise locations and placing them carefully in a box (minus slugs).

After about half an hour, our raking became slower and slower. We were nearing the section that McGurk had started calling The Vital Strip.

He'd even staked it out with string: a right-angled strip about ten feet wide, along the whole of the side of the house and partly along the back. Here is a rough diagram:

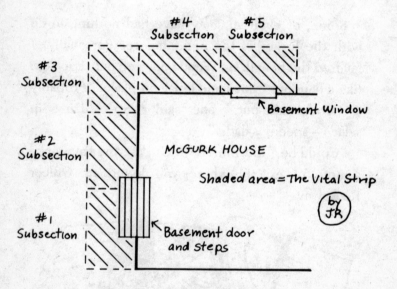

That was the area we did *not* rake. Instead, we searched it inch by inch, standing in a line, shoulder to shoulder—one subsection at a time.

At first, it was disappointing. The wet leaves were pressed down here and there, but those marks could have been made by anyone's feet. Our own, for example, when we'd visited HQ yesterday. It wasn't until we were on our fifth and last sweep that we got lucky.

"Hey!" cried McGurk, stopping about two feet from the wall. "Look!"

The basement window—high above our heads on the inside—was quite low out here. McGurk was pointing to a mixture of wet leaves and earth just in front of it.

"I don't see anything," said Brains.

"Bend down then, like me," said McGurk. "And half close your eyes. Then you will."

He was right. It helped to accentuate the shadows in the two depressions there. Footprints? A better word would have been *imprints*, because—well . . . McGurk had me sketching them on the spot, adding measurements later. Here they are:

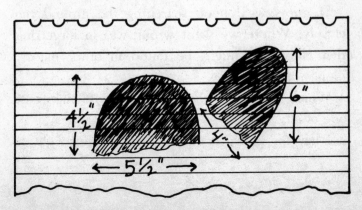

"What do you make of *that*?" murmured McGurk, peering at the actual imprints. "Especially the one on the left?"

"The—uh—front edge of a footprint?" suggested Brains.

"*That* big?" said McGurk. "At that rate, the whole foot would be something like twenty inches long!"

"Mummies do have big feet," said Willie, gazing in awe.

"But one *huge* foot and the other normal size?"

Nobody spoke for a while. We were all trying to imagine whoever (or whatever) could have made the imprints.

Then Wanda sighed.

"It's all very interesting, McGurk. But it isn't getting us much further in solving the mystery, is it?"

McGurk didn't reply. He kept on frowning at the imprints. So did the rest of us, except Wanda.

As she explained later:

"I guess we'd been searching the ground *too* closely. Where we went wrong was in forgetting that clues also might be found in other places, higher up."

Which was where she found the most important one of all.

I haven't shown it on the diagram, but right at

the corner there's an old rambling rose growing close to the wall and spreading out. It was probably Wanda's interest in trees and bushes that attracted her attention.

"You know, someone really ought to prune this rose back before long, McGurk," she was saying. "Otherwise—"

Then she broke off.

"*Uh-oh!*"

We all looked up.

She was pointing to something dangling from one of the spiky twigs. A strip of dirty rag, about ten inches long and two inches wide.

"Don't touch it, Officer Grieg!"

"Don't worry!" muttered Wanda, backing off. "It looks to me like—like a strip of bandage!"

"Very *old* bandage," said Mari.

"*Mummy* bandage?" whispered Willie.

"This," said McGurk, "is where he must have been lurking when we were at the door." He reached up and gingerly detached the strip of yellowish gray cloth from the thorn. "Here, Willie! Take a sniff!"

Willie almost tripped over Brains in his haste to back away.

"A—*smell* it?"

"Sure!" said McGurk. "You keep saying it's a

mummy, so prove it. See if you can catch a whiff of old spices, the sort used for preserving the corpse."

I thought at first that Willie was going to keep backing away. But I guess this was too much of a challenge.

"Sh-sure!" he murmured, cautiously stepping forward. He was gently but rapidly sniffing as he came. Then, a couple of inches away, he stopped. The scared look left his face. "Here—give me that!" He grabbed the strip and gave it a brisk professional sniff. "*That's* no mummy bandage!" he growled, glaring around as if one of *us* had said it was. "That's your regular modern pharmacy bandage."

"You *don't* smell spices, Officer Sandowsky?"

"Nargh! Just medication. Iodoform. Faint, but very distinct to *my* nose."

Willie gave another sniff and handed the bandage to Brains.

"You're right, Willie," said our science expert,

giving it a few light tugs. "A piece of regular elasticized bandage." He grinned. "And whatever else they had in ancient Egypt, they did *not* have rubber."

"Correct!" said Wanda. "Only in ancient South America."

"So it could be a *South American* mummy?" said Willie.

"Baloney!" said McGurk, beating Brains to it. His eyes were bright. "You've got mummies on the brain, Willie. Which is exactly what someone wants you—and all of us—to have. Come here, men. *Now* I know what made these prints."

We clustered around as he pointed to the larger one.

"See that? That wasn't made by a huge foot. That's a normal-sized *knee*print. Next to a normal-sized footprint. The guy had to kneel to peek in at the window, didn't he?"

I began to breathe easier.

"And you think he planted that strip of old bandage deliberately to—"

"Of *course* he did!" said McGurk. "This is just one big hoax." His eyes narrowed. He turned to Wanda. "Hey! How about Ed? Does *he* know about the cat and the guy's story about the curse?"

Wanda's brother, Ed, a high-school senior, is the greatest practical joker in the whole neighborhood.

Wanda was frowning.

"Not as far as *I* know." Then she shook her head. "Anyway, you can forget him."

"Oh, yeah? It's exactly the kind of—"

"I said forget him!" Wanda smiled. "I mean, come on, McGurk! If Ed Grieg had done it, it would've been in a big way. He'd have rented a mummy suit. And *he* wouldn't simply have lurked behind the bush. *He'd* have clumped up to that screen door and shook it and made like to batter it down. Then he'd have had a great big laugh and claimed responsibility."

McGurk was nodding.

"You're right, Officer Grieg. Good thinking!" He turned. "So it has to be someone else, men. Someone with a special reason to scare us. Someone not as good as Ed as a hoaxer, because this one doesn't want it to end with a big laugh. He's much more serious."

"Serious, McGurk?"

"Sure, Officer Sandowsky. So serious that he doesn't dare take the same risks as Ed would."

"But why, Chief McGurk?" Mari was looking puzzled. Also very grave.

"Because," McGurk said slowly, "he has a lot to lose. Or a lot to gain."

"Such as?" said Wanda.

"I don't know. Yet. But I have this strong feeling. And I think we'd better—"

McGurk broke off. He was staring at an approaching newcomer. It was Donny Towers, his beard in even greater disarray and with a wild, worried look in his eyes.

"Hi, McGurk!" he said. "You and your guys busy? I have to talk to you. I—I'd like to hire you."

"Step into the office," said McGurk, leading the way down the steps.

10 Donny's Problem

Donny's behavior at first was very strange.

He wouldn't stay on the chair that McGurk offered him. He kept getting up and pacing and cracking his knuckles.

His pacing made the basement seem dangerously overcrowded. Donny is built more like a professional wrestler than like the social worker he really is. The clump of his feet made me wince.

"Uh, isn't the chair comfortable, Donny?"

"Huh?"

Donny gave McGurk a wild glare. He'd stopped cracking his knuckles. He was tugging at his beard instead.

"Your chair, Donny. Isn't it—uh—comfortable?"

"Chair?" Donny blinked. "Oh, yeah, sure. It's just—well—I'm just thinking how's the best way to put this."

He started pacing again. *Clump! Clump! Clump!* went his feet. *Crack! Crack! Crack!* went his knuckles. Then he took to pausing in front of various things. Like the handcuffs that hung on the wall. Or my typewriter. Or Brains's homemade lie detector. Or the cartons we use for our files. It was like he wanted to reassure himself that we were well equipped for tackling his problem.

But I soon realized he wasn't even *seeing* the things he kept glowering at.

McGurk tried again.

"You—uh—said you had a case?"

"*What*?"

Again the wild glare.

McGurk took a deep breath. He tried to smile, but it looked pretty sickly.

"You said you—uh—wanted to *hire* us?"

The word "hire" seemed to get through. A great, gusty hiss escaped through Donny's whiskers. Then the heavy shoulders sagged. Donny sank onto the chair, his legs outspread and his head down.

"Yes, well . . ." he said gruffly, into his beard.

Then, all at once I guessed what was eating him. The guy was embarrassed!

"It's—" He stopped again. "It's—" Another stop. "As a matter of fact, it's—"

Stop.

With every stop, he was winding us up. Wanda would bend forward. Brains would grab his glasses. Mari, who'd started mouthing Donny's words in sympathy, would stop with her mouth half-open. Willie would press the end of his nose. And McGurk would halt his chair in midrock.

ily—made me look at him closely. "Besides, we have a case already."

Donny snorted.

"Oh, that mummy baloney! I mean, that *shows* what a creep he is! Spinning that kind of a yarn. And Joanne looking like she believed every word! You women," he said, glaring bitterly at Wanda and Mari, "you'll believe anything when a smarmy two-bit jackass like that starts shooting his mouth off!"

Wanda opened her mouth, but McGurk cut in quick.

"Yeah, well. When we've solved the mystery of the mummy and *proved* it's a hoax, that'll make Joanne think differently about him maybe."

A grin began to shine through those badly mauled whiskers.

"Hey! Right! You do that, McGurk, and I'll reward you just like you'd been working direct for me. Hoax, huh?" He glanced at Wanda. "Have you thought about *her* brother, Ed?"

"We're working on it, Donny," said McGurk. "Now, if you don't mind . . ."

Donny left in a much more cheerful frame of mind.

"Well, I for one am starting to wonder about *him*," said Wanda, after the door had been closed.

"Oh?" said McGurk.

"Yes! Like maybe *he's* the prowling mummy. Doing it to prove to Joanne that Keech is dumb for believing all that stuff."

I frowned.

"I doubt it. Don't forget, the mummy—the dark mummy shape—had already appeared to me and Willie before we mentioned it in front of Donny and Joanne and Keech."

"You're right, Officer Rockaway." McGurk's eyes had a very beady look. "But maybe you're not *far* wrong, Officer Grieg."

Wanda sniffed.

"What's that supposed to mean?"

McGurk shrugged.

"Oh, I don't know. . . . It's just—well—let's say that something I've heard in this last half-hour seems to have rung a small bell. It—well—it's just a hunch, that's all."

And that *was* all we could get out of him for the time being.

11 The Human Lie Detector

McGurk had quite a lot to say about other, more routine matters, however.

"Like, for instance, I think we can *definitely* narrow the suspects down to three."

"Like Donny, for one?"

"Correct, Officer Grieg."

"And, of course, Mr. Keech, for another?" said Mari.

"Absolutely."

There was a pause.

"And the third?" said Brains.

McGurk's eyebrows went up.

"Why, Joanne herself!" he said. "Who else?"

"Oh, come *on*, McGurk!" Wanda said. "I can understand why Donny might do it. But what possible reason could *Joanne* have?"

McGurk smiled, rather obnoxiously.

"The opposite of Donny's, of course. To try to prove that Keech *isn't* a dope for believing that old curse stuff. Just to pay Donny back for getting her mad."

"Yes, but—"

"Hold it, Officer Bellingham! The reason I've included Joanne is also based on common sense. Those three—Joanne, Donny, and Keech—were the only outsiders who heard what I said on Friday. About switching the cat to my house."

"I still think Joanne wouldn't do such a thing," said Wanda. "But, yes . . . I see your point, McGurk."

"It's logical, anyway," murmured Brains. "But what motive would *Keech* have?"

McGurk's eyes narrowed to slits.

"Yeah. That's what I'd like to know. Because— well—" He shrugged. "We'll see." He turned. "By the way, Officer Yoshimura, you seemed pretty sure that Keech was one of the three. 'Of course!' you said."

"I did. And I say 'of course' again!"

"But why? Why so *sure*?"

"Because he was telling *lies*!"

"That's what I've been saying all along," said Brains. "A bunch of prime-quality baloney."

"Yes," said Mari, nodding. "But *I* mean in a different way. I mean Class *B* lies."

Everybody stared.

"Class *B*, Officer Yoshimura?"

When Mari replied, it was in a softer tone, but still very firm.

"Yes, Chief McGurk. My ears are very sensitive to voices. As I told Joey."

"But you said Keech was telling—uh—*Class B* lies. What other classes are there?"

"Well—" Mari dipped her head. "Well, my brothers call me The Human Lie Detector. They say I am ten times more sensitive than ordinary electronic lie detectors."

"The Human Lie Detector," murmured McGurk. He seemed to be tasting the words. "Officer Yoshimura, if you're speaking the truth—"

"Oh, yes, Chief McGurk! If you had my ears you would *know* I was. Or at least telling only a Class A lie. The sort that Gerald thinks Mr. Keech was telling."

Brains was all alert. This scientific-sounding talk about *classes* of lies had got him hooked, too.

Even Willie's curiosity had caught fire.

"What—what's a Class A lie, Mari?"

"A Class A, Willie, is when someone makes untrue statement but sincerely believes it is true. A Class B is when someone makes untrue statement or tells untrue story and *knows* it is untrue."

"A *deliberate* lie?" I said.

She nodded.

"Then there is Class C. Which is really a subcategory of Class B."

"I like this!"

"Be quiet, Officer Bellingham! Class C, Mari?"

"Is when someone tells untrue story, knowing it untrue, but joking. Many adults do this, especially when talking to children. And then there is Class D. When someone tells untrue story, knowing it is untrue, but doing it for some serious purpose. People making up stories for their work do this all the time. Fiction writers."

There was a dead silence. McGurk had frozen in the middle of an especially hefty rocking of the chair.

"Officer Yoshimura, this is *great* news! This *is* better than any electronic lie detector."

"Well—"

"Don't interrupt, Officer Bellingham! It's better because, for starters, you can only use the regular kind with the cooperation of the suspect. Whereas with Mari here, we can switch her onto any suspect, any time, without him even *knowing* it!"

Mari blinked.

"Well . . . sometimes people are very clever in controlling voices, Chief McGurk. And I'm sure Gerald—"

"Never mind that now. Listen, Officer Yoshimura, are you *sure* about Keech's voice?"

"Oh, yes—*his*—yes!"

"And it *was* a—uh—Class B lie? He *knew* it wasn't true?"

"Yes."

"But supposing *he* had a serious purpose," I said. "Wouldn't that just as likely be a Class D?"

"No. Not really. Class B—the deliberate lie—is told for *bad* serious purpose. Class D is told for *good* serious purpose."

"Officer Yoshimura, you're beautiful! The Human Lie Detector. Wow!"

No doubt a million new uses McGurk could put Mari's talent to were racing through that fiery head.

"Now that we've got all *that* sorted out, McGurk," said Wanda, "what next?"

He immediately became fully alert again.

"Well, it's obvious, men. Keech is now our Number *One* suspect. The other two aren't cleared yet. But if we can find out more about Keech—find out some possible reason for his lies—then it all might start to click into place."

"But what about *evidence*, McGurk?" I said. "Even if we discover a motive, what concrete evidence do we have that Keech is the prowler?"

"Good thinking, Officer Rockaway! Well, as to evidence"—McGurk glanced at the box of "clues" we'd gathered—"I—uh—I'm working on that."

"*You're* working on it?" said Wanda. "You mean this has something to do with your hunch?"

"You could say that, yeah. Anyway, men, it's nearly lunchtime. After that, I have to go out with my folks."

"Yeah, so do I," said Brains.

"And I," said Wanda.

"Me, too," said Willie.

"So that means we'll have to continue the investigation tomorrow," said McGurk. "Which is just as well, because the next stop is the library, and that isn't open today."

"Library, McGurk?" I said. "You mean *museum*, don't you?"

"I said *library*!" snapped McGurk. Then he softened some. "Naturally, we'll also be looking in at the museum. I have to, anyway."

"*Have* to?"

"Yeah. I guess I was too busy thinking about this mystery last night to bother to hide the cat carefully. Mom saw it and asked me where I'd gotten it and— well—I just had to tell her about keeping it for Joey, so his mom wouldn't see it before her birthday. She liked it so much, she wants me to go get her one just like it."

Wanda grinned.

"*That* should faze the mummy! *Two* cats in the possession of the guys who insulted the goddess!"

"I'm hoping it might do better than that," McGurk said quietly. "I'm hoping it might faze Mr. Keech!"

And that was all he said about that. What he *did* say, as we were leaving, was, "Oh, by the way,

Officer Rockaway, *you're* not going anywhere this afternoon, are you?"

"Well . . . no—"

"Good! I want you to check the Yellow Pages. See if you can find a Fast Freddie listed for anyplace in this area. And if you can't find it there, and you can get hold of a book for any other area, try that, too."

"That could run to an awful lot of entries, McGurk!"

"So what? Just get walking with the fingers, Officer Rockaway!"

12 New Evidence

McGurk called me that evening around nine-thirty.

"Did you find anything about a Fast Freddie, Officer Rockaway?"

I sighed.

"Well, I looked through all the Yellow Pages entries for take-outs, diners, lunch counters, and so on. Not only in this area, but also in New York City and Long Island. My father keeps a bunch of phone books because—"

"Never mind your father's reading habits! Anything about Fast Freddie?"

A sort of lilt kept breaking into his voice. This annoyed me. I decided to make the jerk wait.

"I also looked in all the *White* Pages. I found three Fast Eddies and one Fast Freda. She was a seamstress, specializing in quick alterations. I thought of calling to see if she'd let out the waistbands of any mummy suits lately, but—"

"Cut the fooling, Officer Rockaway! Did you find a Fast Freddie?"

"No. Whoever or whatever he is, he must operate in another part of the country."

"Right!" Now McGurk couldn't contain his triumph any longer. "Fast Freddie's place *is* in another part of the country. In upstate Connecticut. We went to see my Aunt Julie there, in Torrington. It's where they have a bunch of dumb little phone books instead of one big one—"

"Never mind your *aunt's* reading habits, McGurk! Did you find Fast Freddie in any of those books?"

"I sure did!" he said, surging on. "And would you like to know under what heading I found it?"

"Well, under fast food, diners, something like that."

"Huh-uh! I found it under *Motorcycle Dealers!*" This shook me. I'd never thought of looking there. "Motorcycles?"

"Sure! We jumped to conclusions too fast, Officer Rockaway. A bad habit in detectives. Fast Freddie? Ha! It was Too-Fast Wanda, Too-Fast Joey, Too-Fast Willie, and Too-Fast Mari! Heh! heh!"

"Yeah. *And* Too-Fast Jack, remember! Anyway, where was it?"

"Oh, one of those small towns near the Connecticut–Massachusetts border. There was a display ad, same page. It was headed just like the writing on the pencil, except here it was given in full. Are you ready for this?"

"Go ahead," I grunted, trying to sound wearied by his bragging, but not very successfully.

"It said: *Fast Freddie for Speedy Service, Sales* (sales, Joey, not salads) *and Spares.* My aunt let me tear out the page. We can enter it as evidence."

We did. Here is the photocopy I made of the heading:

FAST FREDDIE
for Speedy Service, Sales, and Spares

"But *what* evidence, McGurk?" I said, continuing our conversation.

"Evidence that Keech was the prowler. He must have pulled the pencil out of his pocket accidentally."

"But why *Keech*?"

He made an impatient clucking sound.

"Because, dummy, Keech—when he's not sketching mummies or playing at mummies—is a motorcycle freak. Weren't you listening to what Donny said?"

I bit my lip.

"Well—yes. But—well—there must be thousands of motorcycle freaks in this area."

"Sure! But only one of them is on our list of suspects. Furthermore—well—*think*. Think about the shape you and Willie saw. With the big head and bulky figure and—"

"Hey! Yeah! It could have been someone in motorcycle gear! With the helmet! And—"

"And the big boots, yeah! Also—switching to what *I* saw—with the white cloth face. That wasn't *bandages*! It was probably one of those scarves they wear."

McGurk paused. I thought I caught a purr of great satisfaction. Then he continued, "In the dark, in the shadows, that would be a perfect substitute for a regular mummy outfit. The bulk. The height. The heavy boots. Also a perfect excuse if he'd been spotted by a passerby."

I frowned.

"How?"

"Well, just think of the motorcycle riders who need to find addresses in strange neighborhoods. At all hours of the day or night."

"Mobile cat burglars?"

"Don't get cute, Officer Rockaway! No. Try motorcycle couriers. Delivering packages."

"Uh—well—yes. I suppose—"

"I bet you anything he went on his snooping sessions with a big envelope. And that he kept glancing at it and up at the house numbers. So if anyone happened to see him, they'd think he was a courier."

"Aren't you reaching now, McGurk?"

"Maybe. But however he acted, that snooper would be Keech. You can count on *that*."

I thought about the shape again. It did seem very likely.

"But what about the motive?"

"Ah! That's what we *still* have to find out. And I'm counting on pushing the inquiry further along that route tomorrow."

"At the museum?"

"Yeah. But first at the library, like I said this morning."

He wouldn't say anything more about it then. But I have to admit he'd got me really buzzing. Buzzing so hard that I didn't sleep much *that* night, either.

13 The Greek Connection

"I'll bet that's his."

Brains sounded very confident as he pointed to the big red motorcycle in the library and museum parking lot the next morning. It was beautiful Indian summer weather—perfect for a school holiday—and the machine sparkled red and silver and black in the mellow sunshine.

"What makes you so sure?" McGurk asked, glancing at a couple of other fairly big motorcycles parked nearby. "Why not the BMW, for instance?"

"Well, you heard what Donny said. About Keech's fancy motorcycle. Don't you think that's fancy enough?"

We looked at the machine. None of us remembered seeing it before. Probably we'd all passed it several times lately. But this was the first time we'd visited the museum since linking motorcycles with Keech.

"It's a Kawasaki," said Willie, reading the name. "That's Japanese, isn't it?"

"Yes," said Mari. "My brothers say this is the best. But very expensive."

"It is certainly the fastest production model," said Brains. "With over one hundred bhp at 9,500 revs per minute, it—"

"Expensive, huh?" said McGurk.

"For a motorcycle, yes," said Mari. "Very expensive."

Somehow it seemed to impress McGurk as much as Donny feared it had impressed Joanne.

"McGurk," I said, "we came here to dig for a motive, not to admire expensive motorcycles."

"Huh?" He blinked. "Oh, sure! Let's go, men."

The person in charge of the reference room was Miss Adams. She is a tall, thin lady with a stern face that gets even sterner when she sees a bunch of kids troop into *that* particular room.

"Remember, men, the object of the search is this: *Is the suspect what he says he is?*"

"Keep your voice down, please!"

McGurk, faced with the threat of having an important investigation held up, was all contrite.

"Yes, of course, miss," he whispered, with a squirmy smile. Then he glowered at us. "You heard what Miss Adams said!"

Wanda, who'd never opened her mouth, looked fit to explode. But Miss Adams wasn't fooled anyway. Looking coldly down at McGurk, she said, "Well, what is it you're looking for?"

McGurk gave me a nudge. It had already been decided that in this temple of words, the Organization's word expert would act as spokesman.

"We—we're looking for information about an author, miss. I thought maybe we'd start with—uh— *Contemporary Authors* and—"

"*Which* author? Some mystery writer, I suppose."

Again I felt a nudge. I'd been given strict instructions not to disclose the name.

"It's—well—we know his name begins with a *K*, miss, and I thought—"

"Oh, well, *you* know your way about the shelves, Joey," Miss Adams said. "So long as you, and *only* you, handle the books . . ."

"Sure, miss! Certainly! Of course!" said McGurk. "Stand back, you guys, and let Officer Rockaway have room."

I didn't find Keech's name in the first volume I

tried. Or in the second or third. McGurk began to growl with exasperation.

"Come *on*, Officer Rockaway!" he muttered.

"I can't help it if he isn't in any of them, can I?" I protested.

"Joey!" came Miss Adams's voice. "I'm surprised to hear *you* making a disturbance!"

"Yeah!" grumbled McGurk, scowling at me.

Then Miss Adams came to my assistance.

"If only you'd tell me what *kind* of an author you're interested in, I may be able to help you."

"Well, yes—uh—history. A book about ancient Egypt."

"Fact or fiction?"

"Well, he *claims* it's fact—" Another nudge. "Yes. Fact. Definitely fact."

"Then maybe it will be in here," she said, leading us to a nearby shelf and reaching for a book. "Try it, anyway. And if it is, *try* not to get too carried away, huh?"

I guess Miss Adams isn't really all that much of a grouch, after all. And better yet, her advice was bang on target. As I flipped over the pages of *The Academic Authors Who's Who*, the magic name *Keech* suddenly hit me in the eye.

"There!"

The others crowded closer. I made a copy later, and this is what it said:

> **KEECH, Harrison Purbright.** b. 1947. **M.A.** Ohio State U. Instructor, Ancient History, American School, Athens 1972–74. Visiting Assoc. Professor, Antiquities, Cairo U. 1974–80. Consultant to private collectors, dealers, etc. 1980– . Author: *The Funerary Ornaments of Ancient Egypt*, Amherst Press, 1981.

"Well," I said, "that *was* the title he mentioned."

"And he *will* be about that age," Wanda murmured.

"Yeah!" said McGurk. "If our suspect Keech *is* the same Keech. I mean, if our guy hasn't just *borrowed* this name!"

"No," Mari said, staring at the entry. "I think he is the same man. Positively. Look!" She tapped the name Athens. "The Greek connection!"

"Hey! Of course!" whispered McGurk. "Mari's absolutely right! He's a great improviser, this guy. So what does he do when he realizes we're standing there, behind the door? He decides to say some spooky stuff in a language we're not likely to know, and he falls back on Greek!"

"It certainly did sound weird," murmured Wanda.

"Yes," I said. "And if he was only in Athens for a few years, that's just the sort of basic stuff he'd be sure to learn. Ordering his meals!"

"But we *still* don't have a motive," said Brains.

"Don't worry," said McGurk. "Something tells me we're getting close to discovering it. Come on, men. Next stop, the museum."

On our way, we had to go through the magazine and newspaper room.

"Poor Donny!" Wanda whispered. "He does look miserable."

He hadn't been in there when we'd first passed through. He was sitting with a magazine propped up in front of him, as if he was hiding behind it. It was called *Motorcycle International*.

"He looks like he's on the lookout."

"Yeah. He can see the stairs from here."

"Watching out for Keech and Joanne, I bet."

"Poor Donny!"

"Men," said McGurk, hustling us along, "save your sympathy! We'll soon be putting him out of his misery."

14 Mr. Keech Loses Interest

Harrison Purbright Keech was there as usual, sketching away in a corner. It was almost as if he was part of the exhibition himself. As if, at closing time, he stepped across the ropes and merged with Melvin, going to sleep inside the mummy case.

We were all looking at him with new eyes now. Imagining his long legs thickened out with heavy boots and leather pants. Imagining his trunk and arms likewise given bulk by a leather Windbreaker. Imagining his head encased inside a crash helmet. And imagining (at least, *I* was) his beard wagging behind a white silk scarf as he muttered away in the darkness.

"Don't let him see you all staring at him!" said McGurk in a fierce whisper. "Indirect observation, men! *Indirect!*"

He was too late. Even as McGurk was uttering the last word, Keech looked up, a curious and rather hunted look in his eyes. Then, with a faint smile— the very double of Melvin's—he came across.

We bunched closer together.

"Well," he said softly, "*you* seem to have had some kind of a shock."

He was addressing me.

"No—no, sir," I said. "I—we—"

I glanced at McGurk. He was still staring at Keech as if he was hypnotized. And Keech was still staring at me.

"I suppose you've decided to bring the cat back, after all. Very wise of you." Then he turned to McGurk. "*You* look very uncomfortable, too."

McGurk took a deep breath.

"As a matter of fact," he said, "we *haven't*—uh— he *hasn't* brought the cat back. We—we like it so much, we've come to buy another just—uh—like it."

The man's narrow-eyed scrutiny had caused our leader to falter some. There was a dangerous glint in those eyes just then. Ugly. Distinctly ugly.

"*Just* like it?" he said. "There is no cat on earth

just like that cat. Not now. Not after the curse. However," he continued, looking at me with a sort of sad contempt, "if you're so foolhardy, *on your head be it!*"

Then he went back to the corner and continued sketching.

We looked at each other. Willie was starting to get scared again, I could tell. I didn't feel any too cheerful, either. Wanda gave her head a defiant shake. Mari was staring into space, silently mouthing the man's last words. Brains had his skeptical grin back, though it wobbled slightly. McGurk was frowning.

"Interesting!" he murmured. "There *is* a definite link with the cat, and that's for sure. Anyway, let's get the other one, and we'll discuss the suspect's reaction later."

Up until then, we hadn't paid much attention to the rest of the room. Two or three people were drifting around, stooping to see the exhibits more closely. One woman was at the counter, comparing two of the replicas: the statuette of a falcon and another of a man with a jackal's head.

Joanne wasn't there. Instead, Mr. Evans, the curator, was trying to help the lady choose.

He excused himself and turned to us. He had the look of a guy whose ideas about unaccompanied bunches of kids were roughly in line with Miss Adams's.

"Yes?" he said.

His eyes softened when McGurk placed his order.

"Cat? Sure!" he said. "You're lucky. There are only two left out of the second batch. Very popular indeed."

He took a cat out of its box.

"*Great!*" said McGurk, turning it over in his hand and speaking in an extra-loud voice that made Mr. Evans wince. "It's *exactly* like the other!"

"Of course it is!" said Mr. Evans. "They're all *exact* replicas. And please keep your voice down."

But McGurk was looking across at Keech.

Keech must have heard him, but he didn't look up. He seemed completely uninterested. This was

strange in itself, a total contrast to his fuss when I'd bought the first cat.

"Do you wish to buy it or don't you?" said Mr. Evans.

McGurk gave a start, then handed over his mother's money.

"Yes, please," he said.

"Have *you* thought about one of these cats, ma'am?" Mr. Evans asked the lady as he began wrapping up McGurk's. "There is just one more left."

The lady shook her head.

"I don't like cats. And I'm not sure I care much for these, either."

"Then what about one of the golden bulls?" said the curator. "They really are very beautiful. Would you like me to show you one?"

He finished wrapping McGurk's cat. McGurk picked up the package and was just about to turn away when the lady said,

"Oh, all right! I'll take a look at one."

Well, there was nothing arresting in *those* words. So I was rather shocked when McGurk stood still and gave me one of his red-alert jabs.

Keech was approaching the counter. But fast. Whatever had just been said, it certainly alerted *him*!

Mr. Evans was already unpacking one of the bulls.

"A splendid ornament, that, madam!" said Keech, with his eyes fixed eagerly on the bull.

The woman looked surprised.

Mr. Evans smiled apologetically.

"Mr. Keech is an expert in Egyptian funerary ornaments. Especially interested in the Matravers Collection. He always likes to study the ornaments at the closest possible range, even though they *are* only replicas. Right, Mr. Keech?"

"They're so marvelously accurate!" said Keech, bending to the bull. He put out his soft, white hand. "May I?"

Beaming—maybe sensing a quick sale—Mr. Evans passed the bull to Keech.

"Beautiful!" murmured Keech, turning it over lovingly. "Look at those hooves . . . and the flanks . . . and the way the tail hangs. . . ."

But his voice had started to lose some of its enthusiasm. Maybe the tiny *Replica* stamp at the side of the tail had reminded him that, after all, this was not the original. Even I noticed the change in his voice, and Mari was quick to confirm this, as we drifted to the door.

"He just lost interest. He still admired the workmanship but—well, it became to sound more like regular Class B lie."

She was frowning.

"Are you sure?" said McGurk, with a strange expression—half-triumphant, half-anxious. He had stopped in his tracks. "I mean at *least* about him losing interest?"

"Oh, yes! About that, I am positive. But—"

"Great!" McGurk's eyes were glowing. "Now we *are* getting someplace!"

He wouldn't say where, though. I don't think he himself was really sure right then. In fact, the only place we did get to in the next few minutes was the Fish Fountain, in the garden behind the library. And the only reason we decided to stop off there was because we saw Joanne sitting and scowling at the water, with an open box of untouched sandwiches at her side.

But it was to prove one of our luckiest breaks yet.

15 Breakthrough?

The Fish Fountain is called that for two reasons. In the center of the circular pool there is a large, stone fish that seems to be leaping right out, spouting as it goes. And in the pool itself there are some plump golden carp.

The water isn't very deep, but Joanne was scowling at the fish and the floating leaves and rings and ripples as if she was thinking of drowning herself.

McGurk didn't seem to notice.

"Hi, Joanne!" he said, brightly.

"Hi, McFink!" she snapped.

McGurk stared at her, openmouthed. For a second he looked just like one of the speckled, red gold carp.

"*Fink*, Joanne? Me?"

"Yes, *you*, McGurk!" said Joanne. "All of you! Finks!"

"Hey, Joanne!" said Wanda. "This isn't like you! Why so sore?"

"*You* know why, Wanda Grieg! I heard about that—that *meathead*. Hiring you to spy on me!"

"Donny?" yelped McGurk. "But—"

"Ha! Is *that* his name? I'd forgotten. My name for him from now on is—is *meathead*."

"But, Joanne," said McGurk, "you've got this all wrong. We refused to take his case. Right, men?"

We nodded.

"We threw him out," said Willie.

Joanne looked up then. Briefly. Less angrily. Then she shrugged.

"His *case!*" she jeered. "His case is *being* a case! A *nut* case! Hah! And all because I asked Mr. Keech if I could go for a spin on his motorcycle."

"You *asked* him?" said McGurk.

"Sure. Why not? I'm thinking of buying one myself. Maybe trading this ring for one."

"I didn't know you were interested in motorcycles, Joanne," said Wanda.

"Sure," said Joanne. "I used to go around with a guy who was really sold on them. Before I met Do—uh—meathead. Traveled hundreds of miles. I still have all the equipment. Helmet, leathers, and stuff."

We looked at each other. Joanne had just moved into second place on our list of suspects.

"As for Mr. Keech being interested in *me*—well, you've seen for yourselves. He's far too interested in his work to even *think* of me in that way!"

"Well—"

But Joanne was now getting into her stride. Still with the bitter, hurt, angry look, she continued,

"I mean, Mr. Keech is a *real* expert. If everyone did their jobs as thoroughly as he does, they wouldn't have room in their thick meatheads to go around suspecting innocent people of totally rotten things!"

"You mean the sketching and—"

"Yeah! All day, every day. Sketching those ornaments from every angle. And not being content just to study them from behind the ropes. Begging me for a closer look at them, when no one else is around."

"And you let him?" asked McGurk, *very* beady eyed.

"Sure. After all, they *are* only replicas. You noticed it yourselves, when Joey bought the cat. Mr. Keech simply had to come and get a better look, when I'd unsealed the wrappings. He does that all the time, when someone buys a replica. A fine, conscientious man!"

"Wow!" gasped McGurk.

"Wow *what*?" said Joanne. "What's funny about *that*? Come to think of it, *you're* rather like that yourself, McGurk."

Our leader smirked.

"Well, sure, Joanne. You have to be single-minded when—"

But Joanne was continuing.

"Why, he's even *bought* some of those replicas himself, to take back home and study at close range. That's dedication. *Some* people think he bought them just to impress me, but that's baloney. Pure, jealous-minded, poisonous, meatheaded baloney!"

This must have reminded her of her sandwiches. She glanced down at them.

"Would you—"

"Just a minute, Joanne." McGurk looked terribly excited. "You say Mr. Keech bought some of the replicas himself. Which? How many?"

Joanne frowned.

"Well, I'm not quite sure—"

"One of the cats, for instance?"

Joanne shook her head.

"No. Definitely not a cat. You heard him the other day. I guess he's too worried about the curse. But— well—he bought one of the falcons. And the bust of a king. And one of those god statuettes. Why?"

"Well"—McGurk's smirk reappeared—"like you just said, *I'm* an expert, too. I like to get all the facts. Right, men?"

We nodded—some eagerly, some wearily.

Joanne must have found something amusing in our various expressions. She smiled.

"Why don't you guys help me out with the sandwiches? I'm far too choked up to eat them all myself. There's pastrami on that side and tuna on this."

Willie was already reaching out. Also Wanda.

McGurk slapped Willie's hand and glared at Wanda.

"Not while we're on duty!" Then he turned. "Sorry, Joanne. We have to go. Something important has just come up. Something *very* important."

There was no mistaking the look on his face. McGurk has got as healthy an appetite as any of us. But that look made us *all* forget about food. It was the look of someone who's just found himself on the brink of a breakthrough.

But McGurk still remembered his half promise to an old client.

"Hey—and, Joanne!" he said, before hurrying off. "Don't be so hard on Donny! He isn't *really* as dumb as he's been acting."

"That meathead!" growled Joanne, through a mouthful of pastrami.

But her eyes were shining brighter, and the growl ended in a sigh.

16 Differences

There was still time before our own lunches to go back to HQ and try to discover what was on McGurk's mind.

It didn't take long.

His first act was to bring down my cat and place it beside the one he'd just bought.

"Right, men!" he said. "Think differences."

"Differences?"

"Yes, Officer Sandowsky. Between these two cats."

"But why, McGurk?" said Wanda. "They're supposed to be exactly the same."

"*Supposed* to be," Mari murmured, turning from

one to the other and back again, narrowing her eyes.

"There you are!" said McGurk. "Officer Yoshimura's already onto something!"

"I am not *sure*. . . ." said Mari, slowly. "Maybe it is the light."

She moved her chair to one side and continued her peering from this new angle.

"You see, Officer Grieg," McGurk went on, "Keech *obviously* doesn't think they're exactly alike, even though he says they are. Anyway, never mind what anyone else thinks. Start looking for yourselves. All of you. Then we'll compare notes."

There was silence for a while, broken only by grunts and mumblings, as we bent to inspect the cats closer. Then hands began reaching out to feel the cats or lift them or, in Willie's case, to sniff them.

Results?

Wanda, Mari, and I all thought that *my* cat had a somehow more pleasing look.

Willie, however, thought that McGurk's cat had a more pleasing look.

"Sort of brighter. Also it doesn't smell as bad."

"Oh?" said McGurk.

"Well, yeah," said Willie. "Joey's cat has a smell of mothballs. It's only faint, but I can't stand mothballs."

McGurk's shoulders sagged.

"That's because Joey had it stashed inside his overcoat sleeve, you dummy!"

I nodded.

"Purely circumstantial, Willie. Temporary."

"Yes," said Brains. "And so it could be with the *look* of the cats. Just a matter of slight tarnishing. Joey's has been out of its wrapper for several days. McGurk's has only just been unwrapped." He adjusted his glasses. "Now, a more important difference is the weight. I can't be scientifically accurate, just picking them up, but I could swear Joey's is somewhat heavier."

"I, too, Gerald," said Mari.

"Good work, you two!" said McGurk. "That's exactly what *I* thought!"

But the most significant difference was spotted by only one of us.

Willie.

He'd been sitting, looking a little hurt, ever since McGurk's jeer. Then he blinked, brushed the back of his hand across his damp-looking eyes, and said,

"The sign's different, too. I—I think."

"*Sign*, Officer Sandowsky?" said McGurk, still looking stern at him.

"The—uh—stamp thing. Down by their tails."

McGurk grabbed my cat.

"You must have good eyesight," he muttered, taking out his magnifying glass.

"Yeah, well," said Willie. "Maybe it was the camphor smell, making my eyes water. It made like little magnifying glasses to appear in my eyes."

Some of us gaped. There's never any telling what astonishing ideas that kid will come out with next.

But a bellow from McGurk made us jump.

"He's right, men! You're absolutely right, Officer Sandowsky! There *is* a difference!" He'd been examining his own cat. "Come on! Take a look! One at a time."

So we did—all except Willie, who said there was no need.

And this is what we saw.

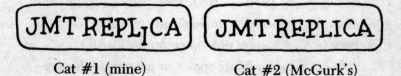

Cat #1 (mine)   Cat #2 (McGurk's)

Exactly alike, save for the dropped letter *I*.

"That should not be!" said Mari.

"Agreed!" said Brains. "The letters should all be alike."

"Unless they were stamped on one letter at a time," said Wanda.

"No way!" said Brains. "Why should they go to all that trouble? Besides, you can tell by the border. All the letters are fixed onto the one stamp."

"Yet Joey's is different," said McGurk. "And why? You can't say the stamp slipped on that one replica. If it had, all the letters would have slipped together. No, men! That was done deliberately! For a secret purpose!"

His face glowed red.

"Secret purpose, McGurk?"

"Yes, Officer Grieg. And a secret *criminal* purpose, too, if I know anything about these things!"

We waited.

"Listen," he said. "This is my hunch. Joanne triggered it just now. Talking about her ring. Remember when she and Donny made clay rabbits for charity, and her ring got stuck accidentally inside one of them? Well—" He leaned back. "*I* think there must be something inside one of these replicas. Joey's. And maybe not there *by accident*!"

"You mean"—Mari spoke in an awed whisper—

"some small but valuable item from the Matravers Collection? A ring, perhaps? Stolen by the men who made the replicas?"

"Exactly! What—what's with *you*, Officer Bellingham?"

Brains was shaking his head.

"I doubt it. First of all, *these* aren't made of clay. It wouldn't be easy to secrete anything in these. And second of all, I was reading in the paper about the Matravers Collection and the replicas. The security in the workshop was terribly strict. Everything borrowed from the strong room had to go right back—counted and checked—after every session."

"You mean there'd have been a big outcry, huh?"

Brains nodded.

"As soon as they realized some item hadn't been returned to the strong room."

"He's right, McGurk," I said. "And please be *sure*, before you start breaking that cat up. It cost me eighteen bucks!"

Reluctantly, McGurk placed it back on the table. Then Brains finished giving his glasses a brisk polishing.

"Listen, McGurk. I know how you must feel. So why don't you let me run some tests in the lab—tests that won't harm the cats."

McGurk's face brightened.

"You mean X rays?"

"Well, no. My lab doesn't run to anything like *that*. But—well—maybe something just as good."

"Sure!" said McGurk. "Let's go!"

Brains looked slightly irritated.

"No, no! Not *now*! These things need arranging. And it's my lunchtime. Mom's going off early to do some shopping in New York. So why don't you all come around at two o'clock? That'll give me time to set up the apparatus. Okay?"

"You try and keep us away, Officer Bellingham!"

17 "Eureka!"

"But—is *this* your laboratory, Gerald?"

We others weren't surprised at Mari's bewilderment when, shortly after two, Brains took us up to his room. Brains himself might have given her a clue when he met us on the doorstep in a white coverall apron of his mother's, about five sizes too big for him. I suppose he meant it to look scientific and businesslike, but although he'd rolled the sleeves up and fastened the belt so that it shortened the apron some, it still looked like what it was. Even with the row of pen clips in the breast pocket, partly covering the inscription: *I ♡ My Kitchen!*

But the room!

We were more used to it than Mari; yet it *still* made us catch our breath.

"Sure!" said Brains. "Now just stand over by the bed and give me room to work."

That in itself was a breathtaking request, because the only standing room appeared to be *on* the bed, if you moved some of the piles of science books and magazines. There were more piles on the floor, with heaps of what looked like old radio and TV parts everywhere. Plus test tubes in rickety racks, and jars of colored powders and liquids.

In fact, the only halfway-tidy space was on and around a small table, where Brains now stood. On the table was a pair of brass scales housed in a large box with glass sides, a notebook, a calculator, and a large, empty glass beaker with numbered measuring lines.

"Brains," said Wanda, "don't you *ever* tidy this room?"

"Sure! I just did. Ready for the tests. . . . Okay, McGurk, pass me the cats."

McGurk handed them over. His cat was in its original wrapper, mine in an old brown bag. It made no difference to Brains. He let wrapping and bag fall to the floor. The cats he placed very carefully on the table.

"Now," he said, "the first move is to weigh them.

Very, very precisely. No guesswork this time."

We watched as he weighed my cat. He picked the brass weights out of a velvet-lined box as if they were jewels. Then, when the balance seemed nearly right, he took a pair of tweezers and started picking out some even smaller weights.

"Why *so* precise, Brains?" I said.

"You'll see," he murmured. He jotted something down. "Now for McGurk's."

Again, he went through the same routine.

"As I thought," he murmured, jotting down that result. "Your cat is 5.125 grams lighter, McGurk. Quite a difference, to say they're supposed to be exactly the same size."

McGurk growled.

"*Are* they, though? *Are* they exactly the same size?"

"That," said Brains, "is what we're going to find out next." He slipped my cat into the left pocket of the coverall and McGurk's into the right. Then he picked up the beaker and notepad and said, "In the bathroom."

"Bathroom?"

"Sure! Follow me."

The pockets with the cats came somewhere around his knees. They slipped even farther down as he stalked ahead.

"Bathroom!" said Willie. "Some lab!"

This stopped Brains. Hitching up his apron, he turned and gave Willie a withering look.

"Let me tell you something, scoffer! One of the greatest scientists of all time, Archimedes the Greek, did his finest work in the bathroom. In fact— anyway, come see for yourself."

In the bathroom, we watched Brains place McGurk's cat in the beaker.

"Our problem today," he said, "is to find out exactly what the volume of these cats is. The precise amount of space they take up. Their *exact* size. And, because they are irregular in shape, you can't measure them with a ruler or tape like you could a box, say. So, what do we do?"

"Listen, Officer Bellingham! We didn't come here to—"

"We do what Archimedes did," said Brains. "We

immerse the irregular body in water."

So saying, our science expert turned on the faucet and started filling the beaker, allowing the water to pour over the cat.

"Hey!" cried McGurk.

Brains slowed down the water and peered closer at the beaker.

"When Archimedes discovered this method, by accident, he leaped out of the tub and yelled *Eureka!*"

"Huh?" said Willie.

"That's Greek for 'I found it!' " said Mari.

Brains was now letting the water drip into the beaker, drop by drop. The level was well over the cat's head by now.

"These lines on the side tell you how many cubic centimeters of water are in the beaker—how many cc's of water plus cat." He turned off the faucet. "There! That's five hundred cc's. So now I take out the cat, very carefully, like so . . . and I let the surplus drops drip off, back into the beaker, like so . . . and then I read what the water level is now."

He peered at the lines.

"Yeah . . . 347. Which means the cat took up five hundred minus 347 cc's, which is—uh—153 cc's. So now," he said, "I do the same for Joey's cat."

"The goddess Bastet isn't going to like *this*!"

"Be quiet, Officer Grieg!"

Brains went through exactly the same routine with my cat. And got exactly the same result: 153 cc's.

"So?" McGurk said.

"So now we are able to calculate exactly what *one* cc of each cat would weigh," Brains said.

He finished drying the cats on a towel and led the way back to his room.

"Why do we need to know *that*?" said Wanda.

Brains was already punching out the numbers.

"Because every metal has its own special weight per cubic centimeter. Like a cc of lead is going to be heavier than a cc of aluminum, right? Well, when I've found the weights per cc for these two cats, all I have to do is look up the number in—uh—that booklet you're standing on, Mari—pass it to me, please—and we can see what metals they're made of."

Brains was punching the calculator all the time he was speaking. Finally, after jotting down the results, he adjusted his glasses, opened the booklet, and began to compare the numbers.

I crossed my fingers when I saw his frown deepen.

"Hmm!"

"What, Officer Bellingham? What's wrong?"

"Your cat, McGurk. It *must* be made of the new

alloy. But travium was invented *after* these charts were compiled. No number for it. Drat!"

"Are you *sure*, Brains?" said Wanda. "I mean, are your calculations—"

"There's nothing wrong with *my* calculations! I— oh, well, let's see what we get for Joey's."

Silence again. More finger crossing.

"Of course," murmured Brains, turning the pages, "if there *is* anything stashed inside, it will make it more difficult to—"

He broke off. He suddenly flushed crimson.

"Hey!" he drawled. "I mean—*wowee!*"

"What? What is it, Officer Bellingham?"

But Brains had turned to me, a look of awe in his wide, blue eyes.

"Joey! You—your cat! It—it's solid gold! Pure, solid gold!"

There were gasps. My head began to spin with the realization that if what Brains had said was true, I must be a millionaire. It kept on spinning with visions of what I could use the money on. Like—

A loud cry shattered my dreams.

"*Eureka!*"

It was McGurk. He'd grabbed my cat and was brandishing it over his head.

"That's it, men!" he yelled. "I've solved it! We've just busted the mystery wide open!"

18 Mari Makes a Call

"But—but I don't understand, McGurk!"

"This, Joey!" He waved the cat. "This isn't a replica at all! And it isn't yours. It belongs in the Matravers strong room. It's the *original* cat!"

"But it has the *Replica* stamp," said Wanda.

"Sure! And it doesn't mean a thing. The one now in the strong room really is a replica. But I bet any money that that one *doesn't* have a stamp!"

"You mean—"

"I mean that's how it was done. Back in the replica workshop. Listen. . . ."

What he said wasn't easy to follow. It was still taking shape in his mind. But out of our leader's

muddled, jumbled sentences, we were able to piece together something like the true story.

There must have been a few of them involved, besides Keech. Certainly one of the craftsmen responsible for molding and stamping the replicas.

"He would be needed to put the faulty stamp with the slipped *I* on the real item—and leave off any stamp at all from one of its replicas. Then the fake would go back in the strong room, and the real one would go with the other replicas to be sold later for a few lousy dollars."

"But what about the checkers?"

"They probably worked in league with the other crooks. Maybe only one of them—"

"But surely they were taking big risk?" said Mari. "That some member of public would buy original. Like Joey."

"Not as big a risk as trying to smuggle them out

of the workshop, Officer Yoshimura! Don't forget, they were probably searched every time they left."

We thought about this for a while. Then:

"So it's been Keech's job to pick up the real ones at the exhibition?" said Wanda.

"Sure. Why not? It wasn't going to be all *that* difficult. For the first few months there was going to be only one place where replicas would be exhibited and sold. Right here at our museum. So—well—all he had to do was find some excuse for being around all the time."

"Yeah!" said Willie. "Getting a real close look at the ones he was sketching."

"And at those that people were buying!" said Brains.

"And doing his best to buy them himself, whenever he spotted one with a slipped *I* stamp," said Wanda.

"But what if he was too late?" said Brains. "Like with Joey's."

"Well," said McGurk, "with some customers, he'd probably only have to suggest they'd get better value if they bought one of the other items. Using his expert opinion. Then he'd buy it himself when they'd gone."

"He didn't use that story with Joey."

"No, Officer Bellingham! Because Mari here gave

him what he thought was a better idea. Trying to scare us. Thinking we'd scare easy, being kids."

"Fat chance!" jeered Willie.

"Yeah, and thinking we'd believe any old hunk of baloney!" said Brains. "Which some of us—"

"Sure, sure!" said Wanda. She turned to McGurk. "But supposing Keech realized he wasn't succeeding? Or wasn't able to make some of those other customers change their minds?"

"Well," McGurk said, "my guess is that he'd just find out their addresses. Then, after a while, the gang would have staged some penny-ante break-in at those houses. And with the stolen property only seeming to add up to a few dollars, no one would be mounting a nationwide search. Anyway, whatever the fine tuning, it was one very cunning caper. And we are now about to bring it to an end!"

"How?" said Wanda. "Call the police?"

"No," said McGurk. "They—uh—they wouldn't believe us."

"They would if we showed them the cat."

"Not at first. They'd have to send it for tests of their own. No, Officer Grieg. The most obvious first step is to check this out with the Matravers Collection people themselves. We'll get them to take a look at their collection and see if their cat is really what they think it is. And also the other things

Joanne mentioned—the falcons and the bust of a king."

"And the bull?" said Willie. "Keech was interested in the bull, too."

"Yeah," said McGurk. "That, too, Officer Sandowsky."

"But how do we get *them* to listen to us?" said Wanda.

"Easy! We phone them." McGurk bent to the wrapping on the floor. "There's a number on the slip in here, somewhere. Yes. Here. We'll call them right now."

"But it's a toll call!" said Brains. "My dad'll have a—"

"Don't worry, Officer Bellingham. It's only about fifteen miles away. And we'll see your father gets the money for it."

"Well, okay. But I still don't see how we can get them to listen. Just a bunch of kids."

"Oh, no?" A broad grin started spreading across McGurk's face. "Mari, *you* started all this. Now's your chance to bring it to a nice, successful end."

"Chief McGurk?"

"Sure! How good are you with a—uh—very serious, highly educated, elderly person's voice? Say a visiting Japanese collector who's looked in on the exhibition and found out just what we've found out.

Who's bought the real cat and realized the one in the strong room has to be a phony."

A smile had spread across Mari's face, too. Then suddenly she frowned, made creases appear, and said in a thin, dry, elderly voice,

"Ah, I see! One who is very concerned to bring facts to notice of true owners of fabulous collection." She gave Brains a cold, elderly stare. "Where is phone, young man? You must take me to it *immediately*!"

Brains gulped.

"Y-yes, ma'am! In—in my father's den. This way, please."

Brains's father had one of those phone devices where you spoke and listened via an amplifier in a box, so that other people in the room could listen in comfort. We were able to hear every word of what came next.

"Hello! Is this the Justin Matravers Trust place, please?" asked Mari, in that same old, dry voice.

"This is the Justin Matravers residence, yes."

The speaker was a woman.

"I Mari Yoshimura from Japan. From city of Osaka where is university." Mari was deliberately stilting her English. "I visiting here and go see your replica exhibition."

The woman softened her own voice.

"Yes? Can I help you? This is Mrs. Matravers, by the way."

"Ah, good! I am glad. I *very* interested in your husband's collection. But I—I have a bad news."

"Oh?"

"Yes. I have in front of me now, here, small cat bought at exhibition."

"Ah, yes, the golden cat replica. But—bad news—uh—Professor Yoshimura?"

McGurk beamed at Mari. Her mention of a university had caused the lady to jump to conclusions, and therefore to listen all the more closely.

"Yes, Mrs. Matravers. I so sorry, but this *not* replica. Is solid gold."

"What?! But—but that can't be! Doesn't it have the replica stamp?"

"Yes. But I fear much that it has been placed there for robbery purpose. Mrs. Matravers, why do you not go and check now? Also golden bull. And falcon. And bust of king."

"I most certainly will! Where are you speaking from?"

"From home of scientist friend. Name—Bellingham."

Brains clapped his hands to his ears, horrified, as Mari went on to give both address and telephone number.

"Thank you, Professor," said Mrs. Matravers. "I will check right away and call you back. Say in twenty minutes. I do hope you're wrong, but—well, thank you for informing me of this."

When the line had gone dead, Brains exploded.

"What if we *are* wrong? What will my father say? Why did you have to give all those details, Mari?"

"Because—because they are true," said Mari.

"They better be!" groaned Brains.

"If Officer Yoshimura hadn't given the number and address, the woman might not have been so quick to respond," said McGurk. "Let's hear what she says when she calls back."

The phone was ringing in less than ten minutes.

"Professor Yoshimura!" The woman sounded breathless. "You—you are absolutely right! Now, can you tell me, please, anything else you've learned?"

"Certainly. One of perpetrators is in museum now. Name—Keech. He—"

"KEECH!" The woman's cry made the box crackle. "H-Harrison Keech? Oh, I can well believe it! My husband was so right to dismiss him! You say he's in the museum *now*?"

"Yes. He is there all day, every day. He—"

"Good! Professor, I don't know how to thank you! But right now I must go and confront that scoundrel myself. I will call you back later."

End of conversation.

"Wow!" said Wanda. "Was *she* steamed up!"

"I wouldn't like to be in Keech's shoes!" said Brains.

"Me, either," I said. "But you should have told her to call the police, Mari."

"Maybe she's calling them now," said McGurk, his eyes shining. "But that's her business. Right now, ours is to get over to the museum and be in at the showdown. It shouldn't take *her* long to get there!"

19 Showdown

In less than ten minutes, we'd reached the library and museum driveway. But, in spite of his eagerness, McGurk stopped at the parking lot.

"Uh-oh!" he exclaimed.

"What?"

"If things get out of hand, the chances are that Keech'll make a break for it!"

"So?"

"So look at that getaway vehicle of his! With *that*, he could lose even a fast patrol car."

"Oh, I don't know." Brains gazed at the shiny Kawasaki. "It's fast but—"

"Well, I *do* know, Officer Bellingham! Think of

the places that thing could go that a car couldn't. Do you think you could immobilize it?"

"Huh?"

"Come on! It shouldn't take you a second to remove a vital part."

"Well—uh—if I could take a look at its instruction manual—"

McGurk kept glancing toward the road.

"Look! Couldn't you let a tire down, for Pete's sake? Punch a hole in it with your knife?"

Brains looked alarmed.

"Me? I—anyway, it might not *work*! They—they look like those special—"

"It's all right, Brains," said Wanda. "I know what to do."

"What?" McGurk stared at her.

She wasn't even looking at the motorcycle. Instead, she was stooping over a nearby bush.

"This should be okay. Japonica. Nice thin twigs and—"

"Officer Grieg!" bellowed McGurk. "This is no time for botanizing!"

Wanda snapped off a twiglet.

"I saw this on TV," she said. "Actually, they used a toothpick. And the lock was a Yale lock. But this should work just as well."

Then she put the sharper, broken end of the twig-let into the ignition keyhole, pushed hard until it was firmly wedged, and broke it off, level with the slot.

"There! No permanent damage. But it should hold him for five or ten minutes, trying to get it out."

"Officer Grieg, that was good thinking! Brilliant thinking! Now let's move, or Mrs. Matravers will be there before us!"

When we entered the museum, all was as quiet and normal as usual.

Well, reasonably normal.

Keech was there, sketching. Two or three visitors were moving around slowly. Melvin was smiling. And Joanne was back at the counter.

That was where the absolutely normal ended, because Donny was there as well, hovering near the counter, behaving like a bearded Jekyll and Hyde. I mean, one second he had a pleading, gentle look as he glanced timidly at Joanne, and the next second he'd be wearing a ferocious scowl as he glanced across at Keech.

Keech was paying no attention to anyone or anything, except the replica of the golden bull he was sketching.

Joanne was wearing a tight smile. Her eyes twinkled when she saw us.

"Why, Donny!" she said. "Here comes your investigating service!"

"They—they—aw, Joanne, won't you *ever* let it rest?"

Donny gave us a look about half the strength of the one he'd been giving Keech, but fierce enough.

McGurk was unperturbed.

"Don't worry, Donny. All will be revealed very soon. Then Joanne will be begging your forgiveness."

"*I*? Beg *his* forgiveness?"

Now Joanne looked really mad.

"McGurk!" groaned Donny. "Why don't you go away? All you're doing is disturbing the—"

But that's when the *real* disturbance started.

Out on the stairs.

A clatter of high heels and a loud voice. Even Miss Adams wouldn't have dared order *that* voice to be kept down!

"I tell you, Mr. Evans, I *insist*!"

And on that last word, Mrs. Matravers entered, with a scared-looking curator.

She was a big woman with a round, plump face and faded blond hair. Most times (as we discovered later) she wore a pleasant, mild expression. But not now. *Now* those baby blue eyes were blazing as they settled on Keech.

"*Keech! You scoundrel!*"

She was holding the twin of the golden bull that Keech had been sketching. Keech saw it and seemed to shrink. His head sank between his shoulders. His beard disappeared behind the sketch block, which he'd instinctively drawn up to guard his face.

Then he rallied. He must have thought that in a modern, small-town museum, nobody was going to spatter anyone's brains around the walls.

"Why! Mrs. Matravers!" he said. "This *is* a surprise! How nice to—"

"Don't you try to sweet-talk *me!*" growled Mrs. Matravers, advancing. She thrust out the bull. "Take a look at *this*! Come on! You're the expert. Give me your opinion about *this*!"

He blinked. I don't think he'd realized yet just what had happened.

"But—but of course! May I?"

Out came the soft, white hand. Into it Mrs. Matravers slapped the golden bull.

"You know where *that* came from, don't you?" said Mrs. Matravers. "No! It's no use looking for the replica stamp. There isn't one."

"But—"

Suddenly, his face went a pasty brownish white.

"Yes!" hissed Mrs. Matravers. "*You* know where that came from! And *you* know it isn't the original!" She turned. "Mr. Evans, you may call the police and tell them we have one of the thieves here, cornered!"

McGurk was in his element.

"You made one mistake, Mr. Keech!" he drawled, in a nice, loud, carrying voice. "You should never have tangled with the McGurk Organization. Mummies coming to life! Kid stuff!"

There was a howl of rage from Keech. He really was in a corner, and, like a rat, he went on the attack.

Something flashed through the air. It was the bull. McGurk ducked just in time. The bull sailed over the rope and hit the mummy case just where Melvin's stomach would have been, if he'd had one.

Keech didn't wait to see what damage he'd done. He thrust Mrs. Matravers to one side.

"Out of the way, you old trout!" he snarled, as the lady went reeling, tottering, and ended up sitting flat on the floor.

Keech was heading for the exit.

Joanne stepped forward, arms outstretched to help Mrs. Matravers.

Keech thrust her aside, too.

"Make way, slut!"

Joanne fell, banging her head against the counter.

With a moan of anguish, Donny ran to her side.

"Are you all right, honey?"

She opened her eyes.

"Oh, yes, Donny! I—oh, Donny!"

"Great!" cried Donny. "Thank heaven for that! Now," he growled, straightening up, "leave that creep to me! Which way?"

"This way!" McGurk sang out. "Down the stairs!" We all went down in a bunch, with Donny gathering speed. "He'll be heading for the parking lot," said McGurk. "Motorcycle. But—but we've managed to—"

We'd reached the outside door. As it swung open, we heard the roar of a motorcycle engine.

"Oh, *no!*" said Wanda. "Don't tell me he's got the twig out *already!*"

But she was wrong. We were just in time to see Keech roaring out of the parking lot—but not on the Kawasaki.

"Hey!" cried Brains. "He's—it's—we—*he's on the BMW!* We immobilized the wrong—"

"Don't worry!" said Donny. "I'll soon catch him on *my* new machine!"

To our horror, Donny was heading for the Kawasaki.

Then, as soon as he reached it, the howls of rage tore through his beard.

"What— Who's—who did *this*?"

"Oh, dear!" Wanda murmured.

Donny was pawing and clawing at the ignition slot. But his huge hands were powerless against that tiny stub of twiglet.

I turned to McGurk. His face was a picture. Title: *Capsized with All Hands, within Sight of Harbor*.

Then he recovered.

"I'm going to call the police, men. Give them a description of the fugitive's *real* vehicle. I'll get them to put out an APB on it."

"Fat chance!" whispered Wanda.

But her fingers were crossed.

20 McGurk Gives a Pep Talk

But Wanda needn't have worried. Keech was apprehended inside the first five minutes. Simply for speeding. They got him as he was entering the freeway.

And, even as he was being booked, the news came through on the patrol-car radio. Then, of course, Keech was arrested on the more serious charges.

It didn't take long for the others to be rounded up. There'd been three more in the plot, one of the workshop craftsmen and two security men.

And it didn't take long to recover the original ornaments. Those that Keech had already bought as replicas were found in his summer cabin in Massachusetts. The cat, of course, we already had in our possession. As for the genuine golden bull, that was still in its package, along with its replicas, behind the museum counter.

There *was* one person involved who was never caught. At least not so far. This was the wealthy collector who'd been prepared to pay handsomely for the stolen ornaments. Keech flatly refused to name him.

"Well, at least he wasn't a snitch," said Wanda, when we heard about this.

"Don't go admiring crooks, Officer Grieg!" said McGurk. "Not for *anything*. Besides, it wasn't because he was dead against snitching. He snitched on those other three pretty quick."

"Well, why was it, then?"

"Because he was too scared." A sinister look crossed McGurk's face. "These wealthy, unscrupulous private collectors have too many opportunities to dispose of the bodies of guys who snitch on them."

"How?"

"By wrapping those bodies in bandages, with spices and embalming fluid, then stuffing them in spare mummy cases. I mean," McGurk went on, quite carried away, "who'd think of looking for present-day victims *there*? I bet there are missing murder victims in mummy cases all over the world!"

We all gaped. I know *I've* never felt the same about Melvin's sealed case ever since McGurk said that.

Anyway, that's all for the crooks. So what about the triumphant detectives?

Well, Mrs. Matravers was tickled pink when she heard of our investigations—especially Mari's call. She had Mari doing that voice again and again until the poor kid grew hoarse. That was when she invited us up to her mansion a few weeks later. She gave

us a bang-up meal and took us into the strong room to see the real treasures.

And, before we left, she offered us each a replica of our choice.

The girls selected jewelry: Wanda, a pair of earrings, and Mari, a pendant. Brains had a fancy for one of the hippos. I chose a falcon. Willie said he'd like the god with the crocodile's head, which I guess was the nearest he could get to someone with a long nose.

McGurk declined.

"No, ma'am. Thanks all the same. The one *I'd* like is the bull."

"So why don't you take one?"

"No, ma'am. I'd prefer the actual bull that the perpetrator threw at me. I know I can't have it yet because it's being used in evidence. But when the court's through—"

"You shall have it, young man."

I asked him about it later.

"Why did it *have* to be that one?"

"Because I want to display it at HQ with a notice saying, *Deadly Weapon That Just Missed Head of Organization, Muttering Mummy Case.*"

But there'd been other notices before that. McGurk had one ready for us, the day after the showdown. He still had egg on his face, then, over the immobilizing of the wrong motorcycle.

"There's been too much jumping the gun in this case! Like I said earlier. Too much jumping to conclusions."

"Maybe," said Wanda. "But there's a positive side, McGurk. How about Mrs. Matravers's jumping to the conclusion that Mari was a professor? *That* worked in our favor."

"Sure! But Mrs. Matravers is a civilian. She isn't a detective. And detectives should *never* jump the gun. Anyway, I've made out this notice and I'm going to pin it up."

Which he did. And this is the very notice, done in his plainer, clearer style of printing:

DON'T JUMP THE THE GUN.

"Right!" he said, after pinning it up. "Read it aloud. One at a time. Starting with you, Officer Grieg!"

With a sigh, Wanda read it aloud.

"Don't jump the gun." (Wearily.)

"Officer Rockaway!"

"Don't jump the gun." (Patiently.)

"Officer Bellingham!"

"Don't jump the gun." (Contemptuously.)

"Officer Yoshimura!"

"Don't jump the gun." (Brightly and politely.)

"Officer Sandowsky!"

"Don't jump the—the—gun." (No. Willie wasn't faltering. Willie was proving that he could be the Organization's most observant officer!) "There's two *the*'s there, McGurk!"

Wanda laughed.

"So there are! What a dumb mistake, McGurk!"

But McGurk was grinning. And there were gasps as it dawned on us who'd *really* made the dumb mistake.

"Terrific, Officer Sandowsky! Full marks! So let that be a lesson to you others. *You* read what you expected to read. Not what was really on the card!"

But he relaxed after that, when the question of what to add to the main Organization notice came up. Usually, we put something like "Bank Robbers Busted" or "Kidnapers Karated," depending on the sort of mystery we'd solved.

"I've taken care of that, too," he said, passing me the extra slip to pin to the door. "I mean, we may make a mess of knocking out motorcycles, men. But with the McGurk Organization on their trail, *mummies* don't stand a chance!"

This notice was in his more usual, curly, boastful style:

Mummies Immobilized